Raider could not risk a shot, not with his compatriots in the line of fire. So he charged...

Doc cried out for him to give it up, but there wasn't much quit inside the big man. A warrior in front of Doc dropped to one knee, lifted a flimsy bow, and notched a short-shafted arrow. Raider didn't see him, or he would never have run squarely into the path of the arrow. The point lodged in the meat of his shoulder.

Raider stopped in his tracks. He looked down at the shard of wood that protruded from his body. The arrow hadn't gone in too deep. It really didn't hurt that bad. He reached for the blood-flecked shaft, but he couldn't seem to get a grip on it.

His head had started to spin. Something on the arrow tip. He looked up at Doc who was saying something he could not hear.

Raider's lips barely moved. "Poison."

Other books by
J.D. HARDIN

BLOOD, SWEAT AND GOLD
THE GOOD, THE BAD, AND THE DEADLY
THE SLICK AND THE DEAD
BULLETS, BUZZARDS, BOXES OF PINE
FACE DOWN IN A COFFIN
THE MAN WHO BIT SNAKES
THE SPIRIT AND THE FLESH
BLOODY SANDS
RAIDER'S HELL
RAIDER'S REVENGE
HARD CHAINS, SOFT WOMEN
RAIDER'S GOLD
SILVER TOMBSTONES
DEATH LODE
COLDHEARTED LADY
GUNFIRE AT SPANISH ROCK
SONS AND SINNERS
DEATH FLOTILLA
SNAKE RIVER RESCUE
THE LONE STAR MASSACRE
BOBBIES, BAUBLES AND BLOOD
BIBLES, BULLETS AND BRIDES
HELLFIRE HIDEAWAY
APACHE GOLD
SASKATCHEWAN RISING
HANGMAN'S NOOSE
BLOODY TIME IN BLACKTOWER
THE MAN WITH NO FACE
THE FIREBRANDS
DOWNRIVER TO HELL
BOUNTY HUNTER
QUEENS OVER DEUCES
CARNIVAL OF DEATH
SATAN'S BARGAIN
THE WYOMING SPECIAL
LEAD-LINED COFFINS
SAN JUAN SHOOT-OUT
THE PECOS DOLLARS
VENGEANCE VALLEY
OUTLAW TRAIL
HOMESTEADER'S REVENGE
TOMBSTONE IN DEADWOOD
THE OZARK OUTLAWS
COLORADO SILVER QUEEN
THE BUFFALO SOLDIER
THE GREAT JEWEL ROBBERY
THE COCHISE COUNTY WAR
APACHE TRAIL
IN THE HEART OF TEXAS
THE COLORADO STING
HELL'S BELLE
CATTLETOWN WAR
THE GHOST MINE
MAXIMILIAN'S GOLD
THE TINCUP RAILROAD WAR
CARSON CITY COLT
GUNS AT BUZZARD BEND
THE RUNAWAY RANCHER
THE LONGEST MANHUNT
THE NORTHLAND MARAUDERS
BLOOD IN THE BIG HATCHETS
THE GENTLEMAN BRAWLER
MURDER ON THE RAILS
IRON TRAIL TO DEATH
THE FORT WORTH CATTLE MYSTERY

BERKLEY BOOKS, NEW YORK

THE ALAMO TREASURE

A Berkley Book/published by arrangement with
the author

PRINTING HISTORY
Berkley edition/November 1986

For information address: The Berkley Publishing Group,
200 Madison Avenue, New York, NY 10016.

ISBN: 0-425-09343-3

A BERKLEY BOOK ® TM 757,375
Berkley Books are published by The Berkley Publishing Group,
200 Madison Avenue, New York, NY 10016.

PRINTED IN THE UNITED STATES OF AMERICA

Dedicated to the memory of Shari Hess,
taken too soon from San Antonio

CHAPTER ONE

"There he is."

Doc Weatherbee dropped the telescope from his right eye. Raider took the glass from his partner raised the lens to look out over the plain. A hot wind stirred sheets of dust to obscure the lone figure that fled from them in the distance. His name was Ceron Lee, and he had done a lot of bad things in San Antonio—like murdering, robbing, and raping the mayor's daughter. Lee was full of the devil. Doc and Raider were hired to bring him back. The San Antonio marshal had brought in Pinkertons because Lee had shot three of his deputies.

The big man from Arkansas surrendered the glass to his partner. "That bay's hobbled, Weatherbee. We can catch him, but we better be careful."

Doc peered toward the sky. "He'll have to stop soon. If he's wounded, as the marshall said, then we won't have any trouble slipping up on him."

Raider pulled his Stetson down over his eyes. Then he reached for the Colt .45 Peacemaker that rested in the black leather holster at his side. His fingers turned the cylinder of the Colt. He was carrying six rounds. With a man like Lee, you always carried six rounds. An empty chamber could mean the difference between collecting your back pay or getting lowered in a pine box.

Doc snapped shut the telescope. "We should do our best to take him alive, Raider. He does have the right to a trial. Even in Texas."

The Colt dropped into the holster. "Yep, I reckon he does. But if he pulls on me, he's gonna think I'm the judge and the jury."

Doc straightened the windblown lapels of his finely tailored suit coat. His pearl-gray derby was pulled down tightly on his forehead to keep it from vanishing into the wind. "Good Lord, Raider, the man is wounded."

"Wounded like a wildcat," the big man replied. "A hurtin' animal is liable to do things you ain't expectin'. It's meaner 'cause it's halfway on to glory and it ain't got nothin' to lose."

Doc realized his hand had strayed into his coat pocket, closing around the pearly grip of his .38 Diamondback. "As usual, your cracker logic has merit, Raider. I shall observe the caution of a professional."

"What?"

"Let's be careful with Lee."

The black-eyed cowboy nodded and moved toward his mount, a chestnut gelding. As he fixed his boot heel in the stirrup, Doc pulled at the reins of his beloved mule, Judith. They had ridden without Doc's Studebaker wagon to save time.

Judith's flank brushed against Raider's backside.

Raider cried out. Judith brayed and lifted her back legs to kick. The big man swung into the saddle, barely escaping the mule's angry hooves. The chestnut took a glancing kick in the side, but it wasn't hurt bad.

"Jesus, Weatherbee, keep that critter's ass away from me. I coulda been killed there."

Doc swung up onto Judith's bare back. "Sorry." He gave Raider a wry smile. "I can't figure out why she doesn't like you. Although, I daresay she does get spooked whenever something touches her flank."

"She just knows I want to shoot her."

Raider urged the chestnut forward. Doc followed the slow pace. They didn't have to hurry. Lee's horse was going lame, and he wasn't in much better shape himself. The plains wind might have posed a problem, but that began to die as the sun disappeared behind the orange western horizon.

• • •

Doc and Raider stood on the crest of a dark ridge, gazing down into the hollow depression where a pinpoint fire burned in the shadows: Ceron Lee's encampment. He was bedding down for the night.

The air was still and cold, a contrast to the day's heat. Night weather could be funny on the plain. No matter what the day brought, the night could turn it around in a heartbeat.

Raider shifted under his leather coat, flexing the fingers of his gun hand. "Wonder where he found enough ground wood to build a fire?"

Doc patted his arms, wishing he had brought along his duster. "I wouldn't mind warming myself beside those flames."

Raider pulled back his coat, uncovering the butt of his Peacemaker. "Maybe we ought to—"

A gunshot rolled over the terrain, rising out of the hollow. Raider's hand was instantly full of the Colt. The loud cracking could have come from Lee's fire, but with the echo it was hard to tell for sure. Another explosion disturbed the cool air.

Raider waited, but the pistol was silent. "He ain't shootin' at us."

Doc nodded. "He shot the bay. It was lame, after all. I suppose it finally gave out."

Raider's black eyes narrowed. He saw a shape creeping next to the fire. The figure seemed to recline in the shadows. It was just too damned dark to see what Lee was really doing.

The gentleman Pinkerton tipped back his derby. "He's retiring for the evening. I daresay we can take him shortly. Have to be quiet, of course. On a night like this you can hear the sagebrush growing."

Raider exhaled, trying to shake off the nagging burn in his chest. "Hell, Doc, this seems too damned easy."

The Diamondback appeared in Doc's hand. "I'm listening, if you have any other suggestions."

Raider hated it when Doc got that patronizing tone in his voice. "He's gonna be walkin' in the mornin', that's all I'm sayin'. It won't be no trouble to corral him if he's on foot."

Doc gave a grand gesture all around him. "Is this dusty plain preferable to a hotel room?"

Raider suddenly had thoughts of warm beds, unwatered

whiskey, and willing women. "Hell, Doc—"

"We can apprehend Lee and be back in San Antonio by day after tomorrow."

"Yeah, I know, Doc. Only—"

The man from Boston was losing patience. "Another of your superstitious hunches. And don't tell me about wounded animals."

Raider shook his head. "I just don't like takin' a man in his sleep. Too much wrong can happen. It's bad luck."

Doc shrugged. "Very well, then I'll go in. You can stay back and cover me."

The big man was frowning. "I still say we ought to wait until mornin'."

"Just be ready with your Winchester. I'll do the rest."

Raider lifted his rifle from the scabbard on his saddle, jacking a round into the chamber. "Go to it, fancy man. I'll be there if you need help."

Doc started slowly toward the fire, heading down into the shadows of the dark Texas night.

When Doc neared the campfire, he perceived the elongated lump of Ceron Lee's body under a tattered army blanket. He also saw the carcass of the dead bay resting in the dirt. The buzzards would have plenty for breakfast—including Lee, if he gave them any resistance. No one in San Antonio would be angry if they brought him back draped over the saddle.

Doc lifted the Diamondback and slid toward the bedroll. The uneven earth forced him to tiptoe, feeling every inch with the sole of his shoe. Lee was deathly still. Perhaps he had surrendered to the wounds inflicted by the marshal and his men, cheating the hangman with a timely passage.

As Doc's hand fell toward the blanket, a rifle kicked up to his left. Slugs cut into the circle of the fire, sending dots of orange embers flying into the dust. Doc lunged for the bedroll, sticking the barrel of the Diamondback into the blanket.

"Don't move, Lee, or you're a dead man." Then he looked back over his shoulder and cried, "Raider, why the hell are you shooting?"

The reply echoed down the slope. "It wasn't me, Doc. I didn't shoot a goddamn thing."

"Then who the hell . . ."

The man from Boston was suddenly aware of the dead weight next to him. He lifted the blanket to see a pile of stones and the saddle from the bay. Again the rifle chattered, peppering the ground around him. Lee was somewhere in the darkness with a Winchester in his hands.

The firing stopped, and a weak voice rose up out of the night. "Pinkerton bastards! You thought you had me. Fooled you, didn't I? I knowed you was behind me since this morning."

Doc peered over the fake bundle, replying with several bursts from his pistol. "Give it up, Lee. You can't get away."

He drew fire from the hostile Winchester, enabling Raider to sight in on the muzzle flashes. Lee had climbed to the other end of the rise, on the same level as the big man. Raider fired three times, trying to hit the black patch where the rifle had flashed. He succeeded in giving away his own position, drawing Lee's repeating answer. Raider started down the slope toward his partner.

Lee turned the Winchester back to the fire. Raider landed with his boots in the flames, kicking out the remaining bits of orange. He scuffled next to Doc, lifting his eyes back toward the rise. Lee seemed to be moving along the ridge in their direction.

Raider cocked his own rifle. "I told ya we shoulda waited until the mornin'. Pretty smart old boy up there."

Doc kept silent, reloading the Diamondback.

Raider slipped three cartridges into the Winchester. "He's movin' good for a cripple. Course, you wouldn't take my word about a wounded critter. I think maybe—"

"You've made your point," Doc replied. "*Mea culpa.*"

Raider figured he didn't have time to ask what *mea culpa* meant. He gestured with the barrel of his rifle. "I'll go up that way. You double back around."

Doc exhaled. "Very well. And Raider . . ."

"Yeah?"

"Sorry."

"Save it, Doc."

They started in separate directions, searching for Ceron Lee as the wind started to pick up, hot and dry from the south.

• • •

Raider stepped sideways up the slope, keeping his eyes focused on the lip of the rise. He didn't figure that Lee was moving fast enough to beat him to the horses. But then a lot of things he had figured weren't too close to the center of the target. He recalled the time he had seen an injured mountain lion leap twenty feet on one hind leg. The Winchester had been enough to stop the cougar, so it would have to do for San Antonio's most flagrant offender.

The wind stopped him a few feet below the edge of the ridge. He couldn't hear a thing with the howling all around him. His boots dug into the earth as he scurried the last few feet to the summit. No rifle to greet him as he came over the top.

He checked the horses immediately. As soon as he approached, Judith swung around and tried to kick him. He managed to jump out of the way before her hooves landed.

Raider grabbed her reins and pointed a finger in her muzzle. "One of these days you're gonna be dinner, Judy, honey."

Doc's infernal mule brayed defiantly, as if she knew that Raider would never harm her; if he did, he'd have to kill Doc as well.

Something moved that wasn't the wind. Judith whined again. The chestnut also spooked and whinnied. A thud in the shadows to his left. Raider illumined the windy night with two bursts from his rifle. He saw the rock tumbling over the dry earth. Then he knew he was in trouble.

Lee's rifle barked behind him. Raider felt the slugs even if they didn't hit him. He dived away from the horses, drawing his Colt as he rolled. He fired off two rounds and crawled in a different direction, expecting the rifle to continue their confrontation.

But Lee didn't reply.

Raider listened to the wind. Judith hollered. Raider jumped up and charged for the horses. Lee was after a mount. Otherwise he would be helpless in the morning—when Raider had wanted to take him anyway!

He slid next to the chestnut, avoiding Judith's wrathful hindquarters.

Black eyes picking out shadows on top of shadows. Lee

didn't seem to be hurt at all. Maybe the marshal had been mouthing off when he bragged about the slug he put in Lee's shoulder. It was easy to talk when something was over and you were giving the dangerous stuff to somebody else.

An invisible shape fluttered in front of him. Raider put two slugs through Lee's empty duster. A metallic laugh as the rifle lever chortled behind him. Raider wheeled, but the chestnut spooked again, bumping him backward onto the ground. He started up with his pistol.

Judith brayed as Lee climbed onto her back.

Raider lifted the Peacemaker with the hammer cocked. As his finger tightened, Judith lashed out again, catching his gun hand with the meat of her hoof. Numbness from fingertips to shoulder.

The big man from Arkansas grabbed his wrist as the Colt flew out of his grip. The pistol hit the ground, exploding harmlessly. Then Ceron Lee dug his spurs into Judith's sides and he was off again into the night.

Raider retrieved his Colt and dropped it into his holster. The chestnut had spooked, but it was still tied up. He jumped into the saddle and turned the horse's head away from the Texas wind. Lee had the advantage. Judith wasn't nearly as tired as the chestnut, and the big man figured Lee knew where he was heading—something you needed to know if you were riding in the dark.

When Doc Weatherbee heard the shooting, he broke into a run. He had climbed to the ridge on a different trail, trying to cut Lee off as he made his way along the summit. The shots were an indication that Lee was moving faster than Doc had anticipated.

He ran a few hundred feet before he heard the final report from Raider's Peacemaker. The sound of hooves stopped him. He raised the Diamondback as a barreling mount flew out of the darkness into his path. The mule came so close that Doc almost collided with her.

"Judith!"

Lee was laughing as he bolted away.

Doc could not risk a shot. He didn't want to hit Judith, even if it meant stopping Lee. He turned around to see Raider galloping toward him on the chestnut gelding.

The big man reined up when he saw Doc. "You see which way he went, Weatherbee?"

Doc pointed with the Diamondback. "Due north. We'll ride double."

Raider shook his head and scowled. "No way, Doc. This gelding ain't got much left. If Lee's to be caught, I'm gonna have to do it all by my lonesome. We did it your way, now I'm gonna do it mine."

"I hardly think procedure calls for—"

"Hell, Doc, you know me. I'll be goin' along just fine, playin' by the rules. Then I get all pissed off and procedure just don't mean a hell of a lot to me."

Doc slipped the pistol into his pocket. "Don't be gone long."

"Just make another fire, and if I ain't back by late mornin', start hoofin' it south, back to Cherokee Bend."

Doc nodded and Raider spurred the chestnut, taking off after Ceron Lee.

The man from Boston lifted his collar against the dust. The wind was still hot. How quickly the night had changed everything. They had surrendered the upper hand in the darkness. But instead of bemoaning Fortune's ever turning wheel, Doc started back down the incline to rekindle the outlaw's extinguished fire.

By dawn, enough rain clouds had gathered overhead to obliterate the rising sun. Raider had run the chestnut through the night, driving blindly in a northerly direction. There was no good way to follow a trail at night, at least without six or seven men and a good supply of torches. The big Pinkerton had to make a few guesses, a couple of dice rolls, drawing to the inside straight.

Lee needed a quick place to hole up. If he kept running toward Oklahoma, he would eventually land at the Colorado River. Raider knew a little sunbaked mud-brick cantina near Richland Falls. It was the perfect place for a tired rat to crawl into the woodwork and lick his wounds.

And if Lee wasn't there, Raider could still have a shot of tequila and a plate of beans. He could wait out the rain that had begun to fall from the puffy gray ceiling of the sky. More surprises from the Texas weather.

He pulled his slicker out of his saddlebag, draping himself with the water-repellent overcoat.

The downpour came without mercy, raising deep puddles in the depressions on the plain. The chestnut gelding lugged along, barely keeping its balance. Raider rode for another hour before he spotted the cantina. He nudged the gelding, but it collapsed under him, flopping into the mud.

The poor thing was ridden out. Raider looked at its legs and then at the glassy texture in the animal's eyes. He hated to shoot it.

"Ol' buddy, are you gonna get back up?"

The gelding's breath fogged the cold air.

"All right, I'll leave you lay."

Raider took off the saddle and slung it over his shoulder. He walked the last half mile to the cantina. When he saw Judith tied to the hitching post, the saddle fell into the earth.

Raider's chest tightened. He reached for his Colt, trying to consider what else he might need to apprehend Lee. His lariat, to tie him up—if he came peaceably. In his waterlogged condition, Raider didn't really care how Lee decided to do things. He hung the lariat over his shoulder and pressed on.

The big man's foot splintered the cottonwood door of the cantina. His eyes focused on the dim light of a single candle. Lee was leaning back against the wall, his foot propped on a wooden chair. He slipped down into the chair, his hands crossed over his chest. Face hidden by the wide brim of a sombrero. Raider gestured with the Colt.

"Let's see them hands on the table, Lee."

The San Antonio madman put his palms down on a huge round gambler's table.

"You're smarter'n I thought," Raider said.

The cantina owner leaned over the bar. "Please, señor, no trouble. I don't like no guns."

Raider nodded toward his quarry. "See, pardner, that all depends on this man here. If he comes along, there ain't gonna be no trouble."

Lee's eyes lifted into the circle of candlelight. He had blood on his face, and for the first time Raider noticed the bloodstain on the shoulder of Lee's coat. He had taken a round. He had been giving them a run for it with only one wing.

A hateful rasping escaped between his lips. "Leave me be, Pinkerton."

"I got my duty, boy. You can pull if you want, but if I was you, I'd raise them hands and come on up out of that chair."

The proprietor wiped his forehead with the back of his hand. "Please, señor, if you want to fight, go out by the river."

Raider kept waiting for a move from the man in the chair. "Let's go, Ceron. You got people back in San Antonio wantin' to see you."

Lee grunted. "Take me fair, cowboy. I'll stand, and we'll draw square up. Deal?"

"The deal is this," Raider replied. "You raise those hands or I plug you before you can—"

Lee moved. His legs lifted the round table. As the tabletop came up, Lee dropped to the floor. Raider fired, but he only splintered two holes in the thin wood of the table.

"No, señor!"

Raider leaned over the table, leading with the Colt. "Lee, you better..."

He wasn't there. A door slammed in back of the cantina. The proprietor pointed toward the exit where Lee had crawled.

"He's out now. Go, señor. Chase him."

Raider broke into a run, heading out into the storm. He saw Lee stumbling through the puddles. Raider followed him, making up the distance with a series of long strides. Lee was heading for the muddy bank of the Colorado. He'd have to give up when he reached the levee.

Lee skittered to a halt, sliding in the soupy mess at the edge of the riverbank. When he saw the frothing river, he spun back toward Raider. His gun hand didn't seem to be wounded. He faced the bag man with his fingers hovering over the butt of an old Remington .44.

Raider lifted his own weapon, shouting over the rain, "Don't be stupid, Ceron."

The dried blood was melting down the outlaw's face. "I'm gonna swing, lawman. That's pretty stupid to me. They gonna wrap a rope necktie around me and drop them trapdoors. I ain't riskin' nothin' if I try to take you now."

Raider's eyes narrowed. "I ain't afraid to drop you, Lee. If you don't start cooperatin', you're gonna be draped over a saddle."

Lee's body tilted forward. "Give me a chance, cowboy. Holster that hogleg and draw on me, showdown-like."

"You know I can't."

Lee gritted his teeth. "Then I'll just have to try you anyway."

His hand fell toward the Remington.

Raider didn't hesitate. He squeezed the trigger of the Peacemaker, firing a round that was meant for Lee's chest. But the man in the sombrero was no longer there.

The mud-bank had collapsed beneath his feet. Lee tumbled backward, slipping down the bank, clawing the mud as he fell straight for the clay-hued torrent of the rain-swelled Colorado. His boots were almost touching the water.

"Help me, Pinkerton!"

Raider hit his belly, extending his hand toward the outlaw. Drowning was a tough way to go, even for a varmint like Lee. Raider felt Lee's muddy fingertips on the back of his hand.

"Almost, boy. Come on."

The big man made a grab for Lee's wrist, but the outlaw's boots slid into the current.

Raider needed something to throw to his adversary.

"The rope, Pinkerton!"

Raider felt the weight of the lariat on his shoulder. He stood up and started to unroll it. Lee screamed. Raider looked down to see him floating in the current. He had been pulled into the rushing water. His sombrero was bobbing up and down.

"Son of a bitch," Raider muttered. "I oughta let him drown."

The big Pinkerton from Arkansas formed a small circle with the lariat. He ran along the bank, keeping his eye on the sombrero. It was almost like trying to rope a calf, maintaining a full run, launching the lasso toward the desperate man in the water.

The lariat kept falling short. Lee went under for a few

seconds. The sombrero floated downstream without him. Raider watched until a white hand came up out of the murky river.

"God's givin' you one last chance, Ceron. I sure hope you got time to repent on the gallows."

He twirled the lasso, flinging the rope with his last ounce of strength. The loop landed perfectly on Lee's hand, dropping over his wrist like a roped fence post. When he tightened back, he felt Lee's weight on the other end of the line. In a few seconds he had him on shore, pressing his boot into Lee's back, driving the water from his lungs. Slowly the waterlogged bundle came to life.

Raider immediately pulled Lee's hands behind his back, hog-tying him. "You ain't goin' nowhere but the gallows, Ceron."

Lee coughed out the last of the river. "I ain't swingin' yet, Pink-man. You just might see a lot more of me before—"

Raider forced his head down into the mud. The big man had never been too big on roughing up prisoners, but Lee was trying his patience. Raider stomped back through the slop toward the spot where the chestnut gelding had collapsed.

The animal was stiff in a huge puddle. He had passed on. Raider felt guilty about not putting the animal out of his misery, but he had figured the chestnut might live. At any rate, he had saved a bullet.

So he dragged Lee back to the cantina. He tried the outlaw to a beam and draped a blanket over him. He wondered if Lee was going to live. He figured Doc could look at the wound when they got back.

The proprietor served Raider a bowl of stew and some tortillas. The big man ate without looking at Lee. He was trying to figure out how to transport the criminal with one horse. They would have to double up on Judith. If Doc had started walking toward Cherokee Bend, they could still catch up to him.

When he had finished his stew, Raider drank a large glass of tequila. He began to feel drowsy, the kind of sleep that could not be fought off. A little nod wouldn't hurt, not with Lee hitched up tight.

He gagged the prisoner to keep him from talking to the cantina owner.

Raider glared at the Mexican man. "He's all tied, amigo, so don't go near him. Even if he looks like he's about to die, you just wake me up. I'm gonna be out, but I'm gonna be sleepin' with my Colt. *Comprende?*"

The man smiled and nodded. *"Si señor.* This hombre I don't even like. He scares me."

Raider set his Colt on his thigh. "Yeah, he oughta. You cut him loose and he's liable to rape you, your family, and any livestock you got handy."

"I would not want that to happen, señor."

Raider's voice trailed off as he nodded out. He slept soundly until the nightmare came over him. He saw Lee escaping into the rain, driving away on Judith's back, outdistancing him on the stormy plain. Raider cried out and lurched forward, almost knocking over the gambler's table.

The Colt fell to the earthen floor. Raider scrambled to pick it up. He turned toward the prisoner, the hammer thumbed back.

Ceron Lee hadn't moved an inch. He was sitting up, glaring at Raider from behind a mat of stringy hair. And the animal glint in Lee's eyes was enough to tell Raider that the wounded cougar from San Antonio could still be a dangerous man.

Doc Weatherbee slept well through the night, at least until the rain started falling. He found an old slicker in the abandoned saddlebag from the dead bay. It was tattered and flea-ridden, but it was better than being entirely soaked.

He huddled under the slicker, alternately looking at his watch and keeping an eye peeled for a tall man and a mule.

By mid-morning, he was sure that Raider wasn't coming.

Doc started walking in the rain. Cherokee Bend was a good half day's ride, so he figured to be on foot for at least a full day. In the Texas rain. Thinking about the loss of his mule didn't help Doc's mood any. He didn't want to consider what Lee might be capable of, even against a man like Raider.

The rain just kept coming. Doc would have welcomed a

hot wind to thaw his bones. He got a cold sheet of water with a few hailstones mixed in.

Then he walked up on the bootmaker.

He was a short, pudgy man with hands that had been darkened by grease from the axle of a stout covered wagon. One wheel was off, and the man seemed to be having a problem with the mechanics of getting it back on. Doc solved the mystery, and in less than five minutes he was riding under a tarp that extended over the wagon seat.

"Name's Sax," the bootmaker said. "Headin' for Cherokee Bend."

Doc nodded. He didn't feel like talking. But the bootmaker did. He began to tell Doc about a widow lady in Amarillo.

With all the things to talk about in the world, Doc could never figure out why men always chose to regale him with tales of their most recent sexual conquests. A man's private life was just that. A gentleman never informed on a lady's reputation. Crude men seemed to find joy in their vile recollections.

"Boy," the bootmaker said, "when I gave her that free heel, she dropped for me and spread 'em wide."

Rain dripped off the brim of Doc's derby.

"Ya hear me, fancy man?"

"Droll," Doc said. "Exceedingly droll."

"Huh? Oh yeah. Ha."

Somewhere in the storm, his partner and his mule were . . . he played games with himself to keep from thinking about it.

Raider stood at the window of the cantina, gazing up at the banks of unrelenting thunderclouds.

Ceron Lee was smiling across the room. "It ain't never gonna let up, big man. Why don't you just let me go?"

"You lookin' to get gagged again?"

Lee laughed and then grimaced in pain. "I can't ride, Pinkman. I'm hurtin'."

Raider held up his Colt. "See this, Ceron? You're gonna be in front of me on that mule, and this bore is gonna be in your back. Your hands are gonna be tied, and if you give me one ounce of shit, you're gonna be picking your asshole out of your chest."

Lee's lips had formed into a smirk. "It's a long way to San Antone, cowboy. You ain't even got me to Cherokee Bend yet. If you're smart you'd let me go now, while you're still alive."

Raider cut the ropes and lifted him from the floor. "Come on, mill-mouth. Time to saddle up."

Lee whined, "But what about a hat?"

"Don't shit your britches, I got somethin' you can use."

Raider dropped three silver dollars on the gambler's table. "For your trouble, amigo. Sorry about the bullet holes."

"Gracias, señor."

As the proprietor scraped the silver from the tabletop, Raider pushed Ceron Lee into the storm. The outlaw faked a pitiful limp, trying to pretend that he couldn't walk. Raider's hand tightened on the butt of the Peacemaker.

"You're breakin' my heart, Ceron."

"I'm tellin' you, Pink, I ain't in no condition to travel. I'm a-hurtin' somethin' awful."

Raider nudged him with the Colt. "I just about had enough of you, Lee. If you ain't in that saddle, you're gonna be lyin' on the ground."

He held Judith's reins while Lee climbed into the saddle taken from the dead chestnut gelding. Raider looped a short piece of rope over Lee's wrists, lashing his hands to the saddle horn. He also tied the outlaw's feet together with a long line underneath Judith's belly.

"Here's your hat, Ceron." Raider draped an empty flour sack over Lee's head, covering his face.

"I can't see, cowboy."

Raider grinned. "How about that."

The big man figured his prisoner would cause less trouble if he was hooded like a hunting hawk. Raider climbed into the saddle behind Lee, drawing the reins around the outlaw's body. Judith spooked for a moment at the double weight, but she settled down when Raider called one of Doc's familiar commands.

"Hell, I don't like it any more than you do, Judith, but we got to do our duty, me and you both."

Lee's voice came out of the flour sack. "Talkin' to a stupid mule . . ."

"Hyah, girl!"

Judith took her cue, pounding the muddy plain toward the south. The rain kept steady throughout the afternoon, but Doc's mule seemed as ready to get home as the man on her back. Surely the Harvard dandy had left for Cherokee Bend by now. Wouldn't he be glad to see his mangy critter returned to his loving possession! What a fool Doc could be.

Late in the day the rain slacked. The air stayed cool, but at least the big drops had stopped falling. Judith kept on in a mist until Raider spotted a group of men ahead of him. They wore new slickers and fine Stetsons. He kept his hand close to his gun as he approached them.

The men stood on the bank of a swollen stream, gazing at the rapid surge of impassable water.

Raider dropped out of the saddle.

"What's the matter?" Lee cried.

"Shut up, boy."

One of the slickered men peered up at Lee. "Your prisoner?"

Raider nodded. "I'm in service to Mr. Pinkerton."

"Texas Rangers," the man replied. "We got one in tow as well."

Raider counted five rangers. "Musta been a' awful mean boy for a bunch of you to guard him."

The ranger tipped back his hat. "Four of us are headin' to Cherokee Bend to catch the steamer to Austin. Looks like we won't be goin' this way."

Raider shook his head. "This stream wasn't here last night."

"Too much rain. Guess we'll have to go around by Lampasas. Want to ride along?"

Raider studied the frothing water. "Might be down by tomorrow."

"Might." The ranger gestured toward the north. "Then again, this thing could turn around and come right back on us."

"Yeah," Raider replied, "or we could get more stuff from the north. Shit. You boys ever have them days?"

The ranger laughed. "All the time, cowboy, all the time."

Lee spoke from under the sack mask. "What's goin' on, big 'un?"

Raider laughed. "Hell, Ceron, we've got five Texas Rangers to ride along with us to Lampasas. Now what do you think about that?"

"Go to hell, Pinkerton. Go straight to hell."

Raider and the rangers all enjoyed a good belly laugh before they mounted up and started off in the rain.

CHAPTER TWO

That evening in Cherokee Bend, Doc parted ways with the bootmaker, trekking through the mist and mud toward the warm light of a well-kept general store. Doc had met the proprietor, a man named Colvin, on his first pass through Cherokee Bend. Colvin was a nervous, portly fellow with a good nature and a young, doe-eyed Cherokee wife.

Colvin seemed genuinely glad to see the man from Boston. "Yore plumb soaked, mister. Git in out of the rain."

Doc removed his derby and gave a short bow. "I must apologize, sir, for my sorry state. My partner and I had a setback. By the way, you haven't seen him hereabouts, have you? You know, a loutish sort with a rough manner. He . . . he might be riding a mule."

Colvin rubbed his fat chin. "No, can't say as I have." He looked at his wife, who also seemed glad to see Doc. "Honey, you seen that big man?"

Her heavy-lidded eyes were focused on Doc. She shook her head, pouting a bit, evoking a deep pain in Doc's weathered body. He returned the gaze, taking her in for a gentleman's moment. Olive skin, thick black hair, black Cherokee eyes, angular features, firm lips, broad nose, proud chin. Her brown curves were covered by a white linen dress, undoubtedly ordered from some eastern catalogue.

Doc pulled his eyes away from her, focusing on the storekeeper. He hadn't meant to offend Colvin by staring at his wife. It had simply happened before he could control it. Colvin seemed undaunted, as if he was used to men staring at her. She would be a welcome sight to any trail-weary traveler.

Doc lifted five silver dollars into the light of several coal lanterns. "I was wondering if you could somehow assist me, Mr. Colvin. I require a bath and some food."

The storekeeper eyed the silver pieces. "There's a tub out back. And I might have a suit that will fit you."

Doc brushed at his lapel. "I'd prefer to have this suit cleaned and pressed—if possible."

Colvin turned back toward his wife. "Nundiayli, get your cousin over here to fix up this man's suit."

She glared at Doc for a moment and then went out the back way.

"Women," Colvin said. "You figure 'em."

Doc decided he would rather figure a bath. The five dollars exchanged hands. Colvin slipped them quickly into his pocket.

"Yessir, make yourself at home. If you want to sleep some, there's a cot upstairs in the loft. And after you git out of the tub, you can have some of my old clothes."

Doc forced a smile. "I intend to remain in the bath until my clothes are ready."

Colvin chuckled and slapped him on the back. "Can't say as I blame you, partner."

He showed Doc through the store, back to the enclosed porch that was used for a bathhouse. The tub was already half full. Nundiayli and her cousin were lifting another huge kettle from the wooden stove. The rushing water sounded like heaven to the gentleman Pinkerton. Steam rose up toward his face, caressing fingers of warmth.

Colvin's wife pointed at him. "Take off clothes."

Doc grimaced. "Ah yes, as soon as you two have gone along your merry way. I mean, you may go. Go. Leave. Savvy?"

The Cherokee girls whispered and giggled.

The tub was calling him. "I told you to go, damn it. I mean it, now. If you don't, I'll undress right in front of you."

Which was obviously what they wanted.

The cousin moved toward him, wrestling to take off his coat. Doc finally gave in, allowing her to remove the garment from his shoulders. He pulled away when she reached for the buttons of his trousers.

"Now see here, my good woman, if you aren't going to give me any privacy, at least allow me the dignity of disrobing myself."

Doc hastily removed everything but his skivvies. When he slipped into the tub, he wriggled out of his underwear, shielding his modesty beneath the steamy water. As he quickly worked up a lather, the women gathered his wet clothes and left him alone.

He felt comfortable with them gone. He never ceased to be amazed at the lack of shame and modesty in certain females west of the Mississippi. Leaning back in the tub, he surrendered to the warmth, which soothed his aches, allowing his mind to wander.

Things had not gone very well. Raider and Judith were lost. Where had he gone wrong? Procedure had been followed. Maybe that was the problem. As Raider often declaimed, procedure could get you in trouble. How was he going to tell the home office that he had botched the entire affair?

A bucket of cold water splashed over his head.

Doc sat up to hear the Cherokee girl laughing behind him.

"Why the devil did you do that?" he exclaimed.

Nundiayli swung around to the side of the tub. "My cousin clean good your clothes."

Her hands worked a bar of soap into a billow of foam.

Doc started to stand up, but he stopped before his torso was completely out of the water. "Damn it, girl, you'd better get out of here. Scatter! Move! Vamoose. If your husband should—"

Her hands slid under the water, groping for Doc's penis. Her presence had evoked a perfectly natural erection. She pushed him down in the tub.

"Quiet, or my husband will hear us."

Doc gave in to her skillful ministrations. She pulled him up and down, slow and fast, torturing him until he released into her palm. She disappeared for a moment and then came back with a washcloth. As she bathed him, small sounds of delight escaped from her lips. Doc expected the storekeeper to appear with a shotgun, but Colvin stayed out of their way.

When he was clean, the girl insisted on drying him and then leading him to a firm cot on the second floor. Doc hid his body under one of Colvin's baggy nightshirts. He required little coaxing to fall prone on the cot.

"Thank you, dear girl . . ."

When she lifted the hem of her white dress, Doc knew they weren't finished. She straddled the cot, stroking him with her hand until they were both ready. Nundiayli guided him into position, accepting his rigid length inside her. Since Doc could no longer move—much less resist—he allowed her to do everything, bringing him quickly to an exhausting climax. When he was spent, she rubbed her hand on his cheek and then she was gone, leaving him to a long nap.

In the late evening, he awoke to find his clothes lying next to the cot. They were perfectly layed out, clean and sharp, as if they had been done in some fine San Francisco laundry. Doc dressed and went downstairs for a cup of coffee and a bowl of stew.

As he was leaning back to light a cigar, the bootmaker came in to join him. Doc found himself oddly in the mood for the man's company. Of course, the squalid little craftsman showed no hesitancy in bringing the conversation around to women.

He winked at Doc. "Get yourself a toss off from that Injun girl."

Doc blushed. "Sir, I hardly think . . ."

"Aw go on, she does it for ever'body. Her husband even knows about it. Charges a' extra dollar for the bath."

Doc puffed on his cheroot, shaking his head. "Hmm." What could he say?

The bootmaker laughed and patted his belly. "Yep, I reckon ol' Colvin is too fat to even put it to her. Course, I ain't never knowed her to give up that little cooter to no one. Probably never will."

"Probably."

Doc was thinking about other things. He called for Colvin, who joined them with a bottle of whiskey. The bootmaker gave up his sordid dialogue.

The whiskey burned, but it put Doc in the frame of mind to consider a few things. "Mr. Colvin, is there a wire nearabouts, a telegraph office?"

"Not yet. What you thinkin'?"

"I'd like to find out if something might have delayed my partner."

The bootmaker nodded. "Could be some flooding."

Doc used the whiskey glasses to make a point map. "So if my partner were coming from the north, he might run into an impasse. Now where would he go if that happened?"

Colvin shifted a glass to the east. "Maybe Lampasas." He chortled.

Doc eyed him. "What?"

"Just a damned rough town, mister. That's all I know."

Doc looked out into the ghostly mist. "Then Lampasas is surely where my partner will go, gentlemen. I'd almost be willing to bet on it."

In the cloudy glow of dusk, Lampasas looked like a piece of rotten wood sticking up out of the plain. The rain-drenched street and moldy planked structures did not promise very much to a tired cowboy. Some of the town lights seemed to grow a little brighter as Raider and his party approached the tiny hamlet, but the big man wasn't enthusiastic about the necessary layover.

The ranger named Brody saw him checking his Colt. "Won't need it, mister. Not with all of us along. You'll see, we'll shake up this place."

Ceron Lee grunted under the flour sack. "I got friends in Lampasas, Pinkerton. You'll get yours, by God."

They rolled on into town, paying no attention to the outlaw's railings. The ranger's prisoner hadn't said a word the whole way. He was a kid, green and scared looking. Raider wondered what he had done to bring so many of them down on him.

"Least this hole has a livery," Brody said. "And a jail, too."

The ranger had been right about everyone stepping lively. Raider had never seen a town so eager to accommodate a bunch of lawmen. Mounts were stabled quickly, including Judith, and the local sheriff offered his twin cells to lock up the two prisoners.

"You sure they'll be okay?" Raider asked Brody.

The ranger nodded. "I'll put a man inside and one out back. We'll watch till tomorrow mornin', and then we got to vamoose."

Raider slung his saddlebags over his shoulder. "I'm takin' your word, Brody. Hell, if you can't trust a ranger, who can you trust?"

Brody laughed. "Me and the rest of my boys will be sleeping in the stable. You're welcome to join us."

Raider nodded toward a dilapidated watering hole called simply the Lampasas Saloon. "I reckon I need to have me somethin' that'll warm me up from the inside out. I'm buyin' if you're wantin', Brody."

"No thanks, Pink. Got my duty, you understand. You feel free to enjoy yourself, though. Texas hospitality."

Raider shook his hand and started through the mist. It was more like hospitality from hell, the big man thought. Low lamps burned over a sawdust floor, barely cutting through the moisture in the air. All eyes turned toward Raider when he pushed through the batwing doors. But then they looked away, because they had heard about the big Pink who had ridden in with the rangers. Everyone in town would be glad when they were gone, but until then the word was out to make them all as happy as possible.

Raider dropped a silver dollar on the bar, evoking a mustachioed smile from the bartender. "Whiskey."

The bartender dropped the bottle in front of Raider. "Hell, pardner, you look as wet as a catfish suckin' crud off the bottom of a green well."

Raider downed a quick shot and then poured himself another. "Wet I am, chief. And I'd like to get a little wetter, if you know what I mean."

The man hesitated behind the bar. A knowing glint in his eyes. "Now let me see, cowboy. You're wettin' your whistle . . ."

"Yes, sir."

"So what else you want to get wet? If it ain't your whistle then it must be your whacker."

Raider nodded. "You know any women around this place that would be willin' to help me out?"

The bartender shrugged. "Maybe. You willin' to pay?"

"Don't we always pay some way or other?"

The man laughed. "Yeah, reckon we do at that."

Raider tipped back his Stetson. "I need a place to bunk for the night."

"That's easy enough. I got a couple of rooms upstairs. Only rent 'em out to the best kind, you know."

"What about the filly?"

The bartender poured Raider's glass full. "Patience, big man. If you wait long enough, somethin'll show."

Something did arrive, in the way of a brunette woman. She was pretty enough, but when Raider met her brown eyes, she looked away from him. He figured she didn't want to take him on. He remembered seeing her in the street when they came into town. Her eyes had been open wide at the spectacle of the lawmen and their prisoners. Sometimes women liked excitement, but Raider wasn't sure he could read her smooth face.

The bartender winked at him. "Your lucky day is here, cowboy."

Raider shrugged. "She don't appear to like me."

"You ain't offered her enough money yet."

The woman beckoned for the bartender, who joined her at the other end of the bar. They talked for a long time, with the woman casting furtive glances in Raider's direction. She still seemed hostile toward him, but in a few minutes the bartender strode back toward the big man.

"All set, cowpoke. She wants five dollars."

Raider threw back the red-eye. "Don't they all."

The bartender stepped beck with a puzzled look in his eyes. "You want it or not?"

"I want it. What about that room?"

The man dropped a key on the bar. "Two bucks."

"A buck and a half and I take the bottle," Raider replied.

"You're a hard man to bargain with."

Raider winked. "Just don't let that whore find out until I've got what I wanted."

He picked up the red-eye and started for the stairs.

"Don't sleep with your boots on," the bartender said. "And watch yourself with that woman."

Raider stopped in his tracks and turned back toward the saloon keeper. "Is there somethin' about this girl you ain't tellin' me, friend?"

The man began to polish the bar with a cloth. "No, but hell, I reckon I couldn't tell a boy like you about women."

Raider glanced back toward the end of the bar. "Where the hell did she go, anyway?"

"Why . . . I reckon to spruce up a little. You know how females are. They's always wantin' to fix things, especially their faces."

"Yeah. I reckon."

Raider suddenly felt funny, like everyone was watching him. As he climbed the stairs he shrugged off the feeling, chalking it up to the big doings in a small town. The few citizens of Lampasas weren't used to a whole lot of commotion.

At the top of the stairs he found a lock that matched the key given to him by the bartender. He was surprised that the room was so clean and dry. He found a candle and several sulphur matches. When the candle was glowing, he reclined on the mattress, expecting it to be corn shucks. Instead it was fine down, another welcome but unforeseen circumstance.

Peering up at the ceiling, Raider mapped out his plan for the next day. He would get up early and buy another horse for Lee. Then they could slip away and make for Cherokee Bend. He wished there was a way to get a message to Doc, but he hadn't seen a wire coming into town. So many jerkwater settlements were springing up in Texas that it was almost impossible to get a telegraph into all of them.

A rustling outside his door snapped Raider's black eyes toward the threshold. He drew his Colt and thumbed back the hammer. "Who's out there?"

A knock on the door.

"Yeah?"

"Are you the cowboy? The Pinkerton?"

The woman. Right on time.

"Just a minute."

Raider slipped his Winchester under the bed, then he hung his Colt on the bedpost near his head.

"I ain't got all day," she called.

"Hold your horses, woman."

When his weapons were in place, Raider let her into the room.

Doc screamed and cried out, sitting up on the cot.

He had been dreaming of Raider and Judith, a nightmare: both of them were mired in the mud and he couldn't pull them out.

The Cherokee woman leaned over and touched his forehead with a cool cloth. "You were talking in your sleep. My husband told me to come and see to you."

He half expected her to grab him again, but she seemed to sense that he was in no mood for loveplay.

Doc pulled his pocket watch from his silk vest, but it had stopped running. "How long have I been asleep?"

"Not long. It's still early."

The rain started again, tapping at first, then sliding into a dull roar. Doc felt feverish and helpless. In the dark dissociation of the night, it seemed the storm would never end.

A lot of men would have said the girl was plain—stringy brunette hair, lusterless eyes, pallid cheeks, weak chin. But in the half-light of the candle she appeared as a vision to Raider, the paid-for arrival of a perfumed angel. She leaned back against the door, her lower lip extended in a lethal pout. Her voice was anything but pleasant.

"Bartender said you'd pay me five dollars if I'se to come up here and do it with you."

Raider put his hands behind his head, leaning back on the pillow. "That what he said?"

She stamped her foot. "Now look here, I don't suck and I don't take it in the behind. You can't treat me rough or mean, and I don't want you slobbering all over me. You understand?"

Raider exhaled, wondering if it was worth the trouble. He was dog-tired. "Look here, lady, I'm too bushed for a bunch of happy horseshit. Maybe we oughta just forget it."

"No!" She hesitated. "I mean, five dollars is five dollars. And I need the money. See I got a man what's . . . well, he's away and I want him to come home."

"Shh. Don't work yourself up over nothin'. What do they call you, anyway?"

"Amy."

Suddenly she was as shy as a schoolgirl. Raider's eyes focused on her large, drooping breasts. He was seized by a sudden urge to treat her kind and gentle.

"Amy. That's a pretty name. Well, Amy, you told me what you don't do, now how's about tellin' me what I'm gonna get for my fin?"

She shifted nervously on the balls of her feet. "I don't know. What do you want?"

"You could start by takin' off them clothes."

Her hands began to fumble with the wooden buttons on the front of her dress.

"Slow-like," Raider said. "No need to be in a hurry."

Her eyes flashed at him in the light of the candle. A surge through her body lifted her breasts. Her fingers trembled on the buttons.

Raider climbed off the bed and stood next to her. He took her hands and looked down into her brown eyes. The poor girl was shivering, like she was scared half to death. Later, Raider would try to figure out where all of his compassion had come from.

He kissed her cheek. "You ain't done much whorin', have you, Amy?"

"Please, don't hurt me."

Raider sighed. "Maybe you oughta just leave."

She shook her head, peering up anxiously into his black eyes. "No! I mean, I need that money."

He gave her five dollars. "Here. I'm kinda whipped, honey. Maybe we can settle up some other time."

He started back toward the bed, wondering why he had suddenly gotten so softhearted. It would be the death of him one day. A man in his line of work didn't get too many chances to be nice.

"Cowboy..."

When he turned toward her, the dress was off her shoulders. Suddenly he wasn't tired anymore. He took in the dark circles of her nipples. The dress hit the floor, and she stood stark naked in front of him, her patch of pubic hair as brown as the hair on her head.

"You sure are pretty, Amy."

"No, I ain't, but thank you for sayin' it."

Raider stripped off his shirt and pants. When he stepped out of his union suit, Amy gasped at the massive length of his erection. She put a hand to her throat and pointed to the whiskey bottle with the other one.

"Give me a shot of that red-eye, cowboy."

Raider obliged her. "Don't fret, honey, it ain't as big as it looks. I got to tell you now, we've come too far to quit."

"I know, I know."

She gulped a mouthful of whiskey. Raider squinted at the girl, unable to figure her. Maybe she was just a young one who had taken to whoring because her man left her and she didn't have anything else to fall back on. Her nervousness seemed to vanish with the second shot of red-eye.

"Goodness, cowboy, where did you get a thing like that?"

"God, I reckon."

She handed him the bottle. Raider took a long slug. He almost choked when she wrapped her hands around his cock. She started to pull, a little too hard. The hands of inexperience, he thought.

"Hey, honey, that ain't a' ax handle."

She was breathing erratically. "It's sure as big as one."

"Maybe we oughta get on the bed."

"Touch me first. Touch my titties."

Raider ran his rough fingers over the tight buds of her nipples. She leaned back against the door, her eyes half closed. Raider lifted her breast to his mouth, tickling her with his tongue and his mustache.

Goose bumps raised on her white flesh. "That feels good,

cowboy. Some men don't know how to treat a woman."

Raider's fingertips strayed down to the sensitive skin of her thighs. She parted her legs, allowing him to fondle the wet folds of her cunt. Raider pulled her close, running his cock between her legs. Amy's body stiffened.

He kissed her ear, whispering, "Don't be afraid, honey."

"It's so big."

"I won't hurt you. I promise. I couldn't harm a woman as sweet as you."

"I ain't that sweet, cowboy."

"I reckon we'll see."

He led her to the bed. Amy stretched out, looking away from him, peering up at the ceiling. Raider hesitated for a moment, stroking her stomach, twirling his fingers in her bush of pubic hair.

His voice had an unusual lilt. "Sometimes a man can go crazy in the saddle. Just thinkin' about a woman he can plumb lose his mind."

Her eyes were turned to one side. "Let's just do it, cowboy."

"Just do it, huh."

His dropped his hand to the crest of her vagina. "Amy, you ever had a man touch you where it counts?"

She raised her eyes to him.

"Yeah, honey, I know about women. I had my fill. Just spread them legs. That's it. Relax. Don't fret none."

At first she was not sure about his manipulations. But in his own clumsy way, Raider had years of experience to draw from, hundreds of nights in the beds of women whose business was pleasure. Amy's face quickly tensed into the grimace of unexpected arousal. He flipped his fingertip back and forth, causing her to squirm.

"What are you doin', cowboy. Ohh . . . stop it . . . stop it . . . don't . . . don't stop . . ."

Tears streaked down her face as she raised her lips to his. The kiss signaled her passion—not the pretend kind, but the anticipation of the real thing. She was no longer worried about the size of Raider's manhood. She only wanted it inside her.

Raider climbed onto the bed, settling into the notch between her legs.

Amy gasped, looking up at him, a desperate frown on her face. "Cowboy, I . . . oh my God . . ."

The head of his prick slipped between the lips of her vagina. Amy cried out and wrapped her arms around his thick shoulders. Raider lowered his hips, gradually filling her with half of his penis. She wasn't as tight as he had anticipated. Before she could protest he was completely inside her.

Amy bit his shoulder. "Slow, Pinkerton. Slow."

They took it easy for a while, but when their motion increased, the bedsprings began to creak.

From the look on her face, Raider thought the girl might die underneath him. He had seen a lot of females in the height of passion, but never had he witnessed the bizzare expression of pleasure/pain in Amy's contorted face. He thought a demon might have gotten loose inside her.

But his moment of distraction passed and he lowered his own head, concentrating on the portion of his body that had given him much pleasure and not a little bit of trouble.

Amy seemed to anticipate his release. She bucked harder, like a bronc with its first taste of a hard rider. The big man from Arkansas met her upward thrusts with powerful exertions of his own.

"Do it, cowboy. Please."

His body collapsed as he climaxed deep within her.

The girl's body shook convulsively, repeating one cascading burst after another. For a moment Raider thought she had taken some sort of fit, but she finally calmed down. He stroked her wispy hair, pecking at her with sweet kisses. She continued to cry, putting her hands over her face.

"You all right, honey."

She nodded, but her sobs did not subside.

"Hey, come on." Raider couldn't stand to see a woman crying, even if she was a five-dollar hooker. "Amy, you want another shot of whiskey?"

She shook her head.

"I mean, there ain't no need to be ashamed. Shucks, honey."

In a weak voice she replied that she felt no shame.

Raider withdrew and rolled over next to her. He felt tired,

not at all like dealing with a distraught female. "Amy, maybe you ought to go on out of here. I hate to see you so—"

"No!" She looked into his eyes. "Let me stay here with you. I got a room, but I hate it there. I'll do it again if you let me stay."

Raider shrugged. "Okay, but we gotta do it in the mornin'. I'm too tuckered to top you again."

She nuzzled her face into his chest. "Thank you, cowboy. Thank you."

For a moment, Raider considered how little he actually knew about women, but then he forgot all about Amy's hot-and-cold nature, drifting instead into the first good sleep he had had in a week.

The rain had stopped.

Raider opened his eyes, peering up at the glow of the sun on the smoky windows of his room. He rolled away from the glare of the light, expecting to touch the woman who had shared his bed through the night. She wasn't there. She had gotten cold feet again. Raider laughed to himself. Women were as changeable as the Texas weather.

Raider muttered under his breath as he swung his legs over the side of the bed. The sleep sure as hell hadn't hurt him, but he was still aching from too many hours on the trail. And Lee was waiting in the sheriff's office, ready to go back to San Antonio, another three days at least.

Raider felt the sun on his back. They wouldn't have to ride in the rain. As he dressed, Raider thought about what he needed to do before they got under way. A new horse, a slicker in case the rain came back, a box of cartridges, a feedbag for Judith . . .

He reached for his holster on the bedpost. His stomach turned over when he didn't feel the weight of his .45-caliber sidearm. The holster was empty.

"That damned bitch!"

Amy had stolen his gun. The Peacemaker was worth a hell of a lot more than five dollars. Dropping to his knees, Raider reached under the bed for his rifle. His hand closed around blue steel. He rattled the lever, cranking a round into the chamber. He planned to find the girl and get his pistol back.

The bartender would know where she was. He was the one who had—

Shots resounded from the street.

Raider stepped to the window and peered down at the entrance to the sheriff's office. The ranger sentry was not in place. Had they left already?

Amy ran out of the jailhouse followed by Ceron Lee. The outlaw had not been lying when he said he had friends in Lampasas. Lee carried Raider's Colt. He hesitated for a moment, looking in both directions. He turned toward the livery with Amy in his steps.

Raider flew down the stairs, through the swinging doors. He saw Lee running along the wooden sidewalk. The big man from Arkansas leveled the Winchester, but the girl was in his sights. They turned into the livery.

Raider ran through the mud, heading for the rear of the stable. He climbed a ladder to the hayloft. When his eyes had adjusted to the dim light of the livery, Raider saw Lee below with the girl. She was pleading with him to take her along.

"Please, Ceron. I can't stand this town no more."

The outlaw chortled. "You'd just slow me down, honey. I'll come back for you when things simmer down."

Raider leaned over with the Winchester. "Things have simmered down right quick, Lee. Don't move if you want to—"

The big man's own Colt barked from below. He dived into the hay, sliding forward on the straw, his momentum carrying him off the hayloft into a stack of hay below. Raider managed to lift the Winchester but he never got it to his shoulder. Lee stared down the barrel of the Colt.

"Give me that rifle, Pinkerton."

Raider was frozen. "You're just gonna kill me if I do."

Lee's finger quivered on the trigger. "I'm gonna kill you if you don't."

Raider forced a smile. "Yeah, you might get six into me—before I get that one into you."

The girl grabbed Lee's arm. "No, Ceron, you're in enough trouble already. Don't kill him."

Lee looked at her, his eyes diverted for the second that

Raider needed. He raised the Winchester and squeezed the trigger—but he didn't hit Lee. When Amy saw the rifle, she swung around in front of the outlaw. The round caught her squarely in the middle of the back. She fell into dirt, dead.

Lee dived toward a stall, barely escaping Raider's rifle burst. The big man rolled off the haystack, landing prone with his rifle shouldered. Judith brayed somewhere in the livery.

"Don't worry, girl, I ain't gonna shoot you. Lee, give it up or I'm gonna have to kill you."

The Colt barked. Raider lowered his head for an instant. Lee broke into a run, bolting for a stall on the opposite side of the barn. Raider took aim, but the outlaw was too quick.

Judith brayed again.

Raider scrambled on his belly toward the haystack.

He saw the Colt come out of the stall.

Then Judith brayed like a demon. A loud crack echoed through the stable. Lee's body hurled through the air and landed next to Raider. The big man pounced on him in an effort to pin him with an old Arkansas wrestling move. But Lee offered no resistance.

Raider looked down at the outlaw's skull, or at least what was left of it. Judith had caught Lee squarely in the back of the head, crushing the bone like an eggshell. Raider had seen enough dead men to know that the gray stuff leaking out of Lee's cranium was his brains.

"Mother of God! What's happened in my stable?"

The liveryman was standing at the front entrance.

Raider stood up, regarding the burly man. "My name's Raider. I'm a Pinkerton agent. I reckon I'm gonna need a hand here. Is there a' undertaker in Lampasas?"

The stable master looked nervous. "Maybe we oughta get the sheriff."

Raider shook his head. "This varmint killed the sheriff. At least I heard gunshots comin' from that way. That boy on the ground was a pretty good shot, so I'm guessin' the sheriff caught one dead-like."

"I'm goin' for the doctor," the liveryman replied. "He does the buryin' around here."

"Shake a leg, pardner. I got places to go."

By the time the liveryman came back with the doctor, a crowd had gathered outside the barn doors. They seemed hostile to Raider, as if they thought somebody should pay for killing one of their hometown girls. Raider picked up his Colt from the floor, keeping it in hand as he explained his story to the doctor. The old man listened, nodding his head.

When Raider had finished the medical man turned back to the crowd. "I can vouch for this Pinkerton. He came in with the rangers that left earlier in the mornin'."

The crowd turned away, disappointed. Raider holstered his Peacemaker. He had cheated them of a hanging, but Ceron Lee had left them with the task of electing a new sheriff, one without bullet holes in his chest.

CHAPTER THREE

After breakfast in the storekeeper's kitchen, Doc visited the structure that passed for a livery in Cherokee Bend. His choices for a mount were limited to a bedraggled harness-bred and a lethargic roan gelding. Something told him to hold off for a few hours. Maybe Raider would show by then. At least the big man knew where his partner was, which was more than the gentleman Pinkerton could say.

On the porch of the general store, Doc found a comfortable wooden chair and a cool prairie breeze. He torched the end of a fresh Old Virginia cheroot, enjoying a good smoke in the shade of the wooden veranda. His eyes stared into the north-eastern horizon, the direction Raider would ride in from if he came from Lampasas.

Doc wished he had been in possession of his maps. Then he would have been able to calculate the distance and a possible arrival time for his partner. Of course, he was guessing that Raider had captured Lee—a giant assumption. There was no way to tell how long Raider would go before he caught up to the outlaw. Sometimes the man from Arkansas would be gone for weeks in pursuit of a criminal. One thing Doc was sure of—barring death, Raider would not stop until he found his quarry.

By late afternoon, Doc had decided to stay another night in Colvin's loft. He'd wait until noon the next day and then buy one of the mounts. Austin would be the closest place to get off a telegram to the home office. He needed expense money and a train ticket back to San Antonio.

Doc exhaled and peered out into the growing shadows on the plain. "Damn you, you river-running hillbilly, why don't you just ride in here and put my mind at ease?"

But by suppertime there was no sign of Raider. Doc sat in the general store, sipping coffee, gazing out the window, refusing to entertain thoughts of Raider's demise. He expected his partner to come winding down the dark street at any moment.

Doc perked up when two burly men approached the store. He slipped back down in his chair when they came into the light. It wasn't Raider and Lee. Instead, a buckskinned man and a man in a gray duster hitched their mounts in front of Colvin's establishment.

They were rough-looking, but Doc didn't pay much attention to them until he noticed the storekeeper's nervous reaction. Colvin's manner was short, clipped, as if he knew the two men and wanted them out of his place before there was any trouble. Doc pushed away from the table by the window, staying in his chair but making sure he had easy access to his Diamondback.

The grizzle-faced man with the buckskin coat leaned over the counter toward the proprietor. "How's that squaw of yourn, Colvin?"

Doc's host smiled weakly. "Well, er, she's took up with the grippe somethin' awful, yessiree."

The man in the dark-stained duster gave a hateful laugh. "Too bad. I need somebody to wash my back. No chance for a bath, huh?"

Colvin eased away from the counter. "Now look here, Milo. I don't want no—"

Milo, the buckskinned man, grabbed the front of Colvin's shirt. "You tell that squaw to git out of bed and draw us a bath."

"I ain't havin' it like last time, Milo," Colvin cried.

"Then what are you gonna do about it? Huh?" Milo pushed him back. "You ain't gonna do shit. You got that. Ain't nobody gonna do shit." He made the mistake of turning toward

Doc. "You ain't gonna do shit, are you, dandy? Huh? Hey, I'm talkin' to you, son."

Doc stood up slowly. "Sir, I suggest you unhand that gentleman and take your business elsewhere."

Milo grinned dumbly, as if he could not believe that Doc had challenged him so quickly. "What'd you say, boy?"

Doc stepped forward, marking the Buntline on Milo's hip. The man in the duster had drawn back his coat, uncovering an old Navy Colt. If it came to blows, he'd have to be quick with the Diamondback. Doc planned to deal peaceably with them as long as he had a choice.

"Mr. Milo, I simply remarked that you would be wise to let go of Mr. Colvin's shirt and vacate the premises."

The man in the duster grinned at his partner. "Hear that, Milo? He simplee ree-marked. Haw, haw. How 'bout that?"

Doc sighed, thinking to himself that ignorance in any form was never very refreshing, especially when it took the shape of a bully.

Milo put a finger in Doc's face. "I got me a gun, fancy pants. What you gonna do if I use it on you?"

"That," Doc replied, "is something for which I cannot be held responsible. Colvin, you're a witness. These men threatened me."

Milo snatched Doc's derby off his head. "I got me a fancy hat. And there ain't nothin' you can—ahh!"

Doc had grabbed Milo's wrist, applying pressure that caused the ruffian to release his hold on the derby.

Milo sank to the floor on one knee. Doc kicked him in the chest, sending him back toward the counter. The man in the duster moved, but he never drew his gun. A loud blast resounded to Doc's left. Raider stood in the doorway with his smoking Colt in hand.

"Son of a bitch, Weatherbee. I leave you alone for a couple of days and you just have to go out and get into trouble."

The man in the duster was holding his wrist where Raider had shot him. "You winged me, damn you. Milo, he winged me."

Raider gestured with the barrel of the Colt. "You better thank your Maker that I've had enough of killin' these days."

Milo groaned as he stirred on the floor. "What happened?"

Doc helped him to his feet. "You were simply bested by a superior opponent, my friend. Now I suggest you leave before my associate here decides to resume his gunslinging ways."

Milo frowned at Raider. "Listen, boys, hey, I'm sorry about the . . . I mean, I ain't lookin' for no trouble."

Raider showed them to the door. "And don't be tryin' to backshoot us."

"I think they was Pinkertons," said the wounded man in the duster.

"Shut up and ride."

Raider started to close the door. Judith brayed at the hitching post outside. The man from Boston flew out into the street and wrapped his arms around Judith's neck.

Raider shook his head, turning to the storekeeper. "You ever see a man so crazy about a mule?"

Colvin was looking wide-eyed at Raider's Colt.

"Aw, don't fret none," the big man said, holstering the sidearm. "I ain't gonna shoot you. And if them boys come back, you just make sure you got a shotgun behind the counter."

"Yes, sir."

Doc came back inside, rubbing his hands together. "I'll need a feedbag, some oats, and a grooming brush."

Colvin nodded and started for his storeroom.

"I'm ready to put on the feedbag myself," Raider said. "Hell, Doc, you wouldna believed the mud between here and Lampasas."

Doc gestured toward his mule. "I see you dispatched Lee into the netherworld. What did you hit him with?"

"Thank Judith for that. She kicked the pee-livin' life out of him. Crushed his skull. Good shot, too."

Colvin came back with the feedbag. Doc went outside to tend to his beloved beast of burden. The storekeeper disappeared, only to return with a steaming bowl of stew for Raider.

Colvin shook his head as the big man ate. "Y'all sure do know how to stir up a ruckus."

Raider laughed, shoving a biscuit into his mouth. "Yeah, well, just between you and me, I'm ready for San Antone, pardner. I'm just real goddamn tired of ridin' wild asses through the dirt and mud."

Colvin smiled. "I can see what you mean, cowboy."

Raider turned halfway toward the storekeeper. "Maybe you oughta just have your squaw draw me a bath."

"That I can do, sir, that I can do."

"And maybe you can git me a shot of whiskey?"

"Corn liquor all right?"

Raider nodded. He would have drunk horse liniment if it meant a little warmth in his bones. As he pushed away from the table, he prayed that the stories about Colvin's squaw were true.

Raider eased himself down into the steaming tub. The hot water made him feel weak, as if his body had failed him. He closed his eyes and tried not to think about the ride to San Antonio. Doc would probably want to head out right away.

"You damned cowboy. How did you get in here without me seeing you?"

Raider looked up into the brown eyes of Colvin's wife, Nundiayli. "Sorry, ma'am. I just seen this bathtub and I plumb lost my head."

She offered a half smile on her thick coral lips.

The big man smiled himself. "Say, you sure are a pretty one. I bet you're Cherokee."

Nundiayli nodded. "I come from Oklahoma."

"Listen, honey, I ain't got time to waste words, so I'm just gonna put it to you blunt-like." He hesitated, trying to find the right phrase. "Er, they say that you, well . . . just that you got a way of relievin' a fella if he needs to be . . ."

She put a finger to her lips. "Don't let my husband hear you." She slid closer to the tub, kneeling beside Raider. He felt his body stiffen when she laved her hands in the water. She rolled up a heavy lather between her palms, all the time looking straight into Raider's eyes.

"You look tired, cowboy."

He nodded. "Yep, I reckon I . . ."

Her fingers had found their target between his legs.

Nundiayli suddenly wore an expression of delight and puzzlement. She giggled and went to work on him, causing him to rise up out of the water. Raider held on to the edges of the tub, cringing with pleasure.

He ran one hand along the tub to Nundiayli's shoulder. "Git on in this water with me, woman."

But she drew away, keeping him between her hands. Raider quickly surrendered to her stroking. He closed his eyes, losing himself in his imaginings, allowing the Cherokee woman to bring him to his summit. She let go of him as soon as he had discharged.

"Hey, woman, where you goin'?"

She shrugged. "Downstairs."

"Well, look here. You go git me a new pair of denims, a long-sleeve shirt, a pair of socks, and a new union suit. My partner'll give you the money. And tell your hubby to fish me out a box of forty-five cartridges, too."

He sighed as she sashayed out of the bathhouse. He could have done her again, his way. Of course, the rumors had it that she never went down for anyone, but only gave the jerk job in the tub. Some said her husband knew and didn't care, others said he was just too dumb to catch on.

Raider finished soaking and stood up to towel himself off. He heard more giggling behind him. Nundiayli had come back with her cousin. The girl was eyeing Raider's semi-turgid member.

"Tell her she can have it for free," the big man said.

The cousin nodded. Nundiayli gestured for Raider to follow her. He wrapped the towel around himself and dogged the footsteps of both Cherokee women. Colvin's wife led them to her own bedroom, complete with a goose-down mattress. She closed the door, leaving the big man alone with her cousin.

Before Raider could say a word, the girl was stripped and lying back on the comforter. He didn't need any coaxing. His cock sprang to life immediately, searching for a home between the girl's legs.

When they had finished shaking the bedsprings, the girl jumped off the bed and slipped on her cotton dress. Raider watched her as she fled from the bedroom, leaving him alone in the storekeeper's bed. He suddenly had a funny feeling in his gut. What if Colvin found him naked between the sheets? What would Raider say?

The door cracked open slightly. The big man's stomach turned over. He exhaled when Nundiayli stuck her head through the threshold.

"Jesus, woman, you scared the hell out of me."

She threw several pieces of clothing onto the bed. "You wanted something to dress up in, here you go."

Raider touched the new fabric. "I'll be warm in these."

Nundiayli gave him a look when he climbed off the mattress.

Raider grinned. "You sure you don't want to try it?"

She turned her back to him.

The big man shrugged and slipped into his fresh change of clothes. She had brought his boots as well. They had been drying by the stove downstairs.

"I blocked out your hat, cowboy. It's in the kitchen."

The big man looked over his shoulder into her brown eyes. "You're just one hell of a woman to have around, sweetheart."

At that particularly awkward moment, Colvin burst into the bedroom. He cast a quizzical glance in Raider's direction. It didn't help that the big Pinkerton was perched on the edge of the bed. He stood up quickly, trying not to look too guilty.

"Er . . . howdy, sir. She, I mean, your wife here done let me change my clothes back here. It was so damned cold on that porch . . ."

Colvin nodded. "I see. Nundiayli, I need your help. Mr. Raider, your partner wishes to see you."

With that, they all three exited the bedchamber. Raider joined Doc at the table by the window. The man from Boston was having coffee; Raider opted for a bottle of red-eye.

Doc gazed out toward his beloved mule. "Raider, I must thank you for bringing Judith back to me."

"Aw, don't start up. Next thing you know, you'll want to be gettin' a marriage license for that critter."

Doc turned to look his partner in the eye. "About the report . . . I must mention that I was negligent in my—"

"Doc, put a stopper in it. I don't care nothin' about no report. You just say what you want. Say *you* caught Lee if you want to. But don't spend no hours frettin' 'cause we had some complications. Hell, it wouldn't be right if somethin' didn't go wrong."

Doc's eyes narrowed. "Your logic escapes me."

Raider snorted and folded his arms over his chest. "Doc, do you really think anybody at the home office gives two hoots in hell if we tell 'em anything but 'case closed'?"

"Mr. Pinkerton requires detailed reports."

"So if anybody's killed, we've got our butts covered. Sheeit, we come in and gut the carcass and ever'body else get to take home the meat."

"Nevertheless, I shall be detailed and accurate. Nothing will stop me from reporting the truth."

Raider grinned. "You gonna report about the bathhouse squaw?"

Doc turned two shades of red. "I don't know what you're talking about."

"Haw, haw. I knew it. You wouldn't come to a place like this without gettin' yourself a bath."

Doc considered reaching for his Diamondback. "One more word . . ."

"Doc, did you have a bath?"

"I had considerably more!"

Raider gawked at him. "You don't mean . . . she gave *it* up to you. She never gave it up to anybody. You're a goddamn legend, Doc, a goddamn legend."

The man from Boston slammed his Diamondback on the table. "If you want to say something else, say it to my weapon."

"Hell, Doc, I was just—"

"We ride out tonight. Unless you have any objections."

Raider laughed. "Since you put it like that, I'm all for gettin' this thing over with. And you know what, Doc?"

"No, what?"

"I bet ol' Ceron Lee don't have any objections either."

"There she is, Doc. San Antone!"

Allan Pinkerton's finest pair of detectives had stopped on the edge of the plateau to gaze south toward the sprawling

Texas town that rose up out of the plain like an unexpected oasis. The three-day ride had gone quickly, even though Raider was forced to ride one of the nags purchased in Cherokee Bend. Doc shifted on Judith's back. The dead outlaw had been strung over the shoulders of another swaybacked steed.

Raider slapped his thigh. "Dang it, I sure do like San Antone."

Doc fished for an Old Virginia cheroot, the one he had been saving for the end of the trail. "Yes, San Antonio has been around for quite a while."

"This gonna be a history lesson?"

"Founded by the Spanish more than a hundred years ago. Of course, we won it back in the Mexican War. That was almost forty years ago."

Raider scowled, hoping Doc would not be too long-winded. "Yeah, ol' Jim Bowie and Davy Crockett done the Alamo right proud."

"Look at her now. A bustling center of civilized activity. Rails and cattle. The beginning of the Chisholm Trail."

Raider sighed, remembering something from his past. "Yeah, I rode a couple of trail drives to Kansas City myself when I was a pup. Hell, these trains are gonna kill the trail sooner or later, just like they done with ever'thing else."

Doc shrugged. He struck a match and torched the end of his cheroot. "We can't stop progress, Raider."

The big man looked back at the body of Ceron Lee. "Can't stop him from stinkin', either, Weatherbee." He pointed to the clear sky. "Buzzards been circlin' us all mornin'. Ol' Ceron is gettin' kinda gamey."

Doc pulled his Diamondback from his coat pocket. "Allow me to send them on their way."

"No!" Raider tipped back his Stetson. "I mean, you might hit one, Doc, and shootin' a buzzard can be bad luck." His eyes traced the patterns as the scavengers soared effortlessly overhead on hot air currents. "Besides, they keep the countryside picked clean. You wanna bet how bad it'd stink if they's to kill all the buzzards?"

The man from Boston reluctantly put his gun away. "I suppose you're right. They rather give me a nervous feeling. As if something bad were going to happen."

Raider nodded toward Lee's body. "Looks like it's already happened to ol' Ceron there."

Doc felt a shiver through his shoulders. "I don't think I'll ever grow accustomed to death."

"That's 'cause you know them vultures is gonna be pickin' at our bones one day. Ain't that it, Doc?"

On that cheery note, Doc urged Judith forward. Raider followed on the broken-down mount, trying to keep pace with his partner as they drew closer to the city. They were silent for a long time before the big man spoke again.

"Yeah, Weatherbee, I think the worst is over, at least for the time bein'. Somethin' tells me we're gonna have a whale of a time in San Antone."

Doc raised a cautious eyebrow. "Wasn't Jonah swallowed by a whale?"

"Hey, Doc, I been meanin' to tell you somethin' for a long time."

"And what might that be?"

"Just shut up, partner. Just shut the hell up."

They spent their first hour in San Antonio smoothing out the ragged edges. The marshal was not all displeased to see the return of an inanimate Ceron Lee. The town undertaker quickly dispatched the spoiling carcass to "the badman's field." Officials in San Antonio were on a drive to rid the central Texas municipality of undesirable citizens.

Doc and Raider declined the reward money, telling the marshal to disperse the bounty to the families of the three deputies killed in the line of duty by Lee's gun hand. They just wanted to take care of their personal and Pinkerton business, and then sleep until the home office sent them after some other law-breaking madman.

Raider figured Doc was going to be a pain in the butt, so the big man tried to get away from him after they had stabled Judith and the other two hayburners. But the gentleman detective dogged his partner's long steps all the way back to the hotel, insisting vehemently that they should write their report as soon as possible, while everything was still fresh in their minds. Telegrams to the home office were in order as well.

Raider surrendered to Doc's efficiency, but not before he bought a bottle of good Irish whiskey to accompany him upstairs.

Doc sat down at a small desk and started writing. They went over the pursuit and capture of Ceron Lee, with Doc scrawling every detail. Raider thought his partner was going too far in blaming himself for Lee's last-ditch escape attempt. But the big man didn't want to prolong the agony, so he just kept his mouth shut and threw back another shot of Irish rye. His face was starting to glow a little. He felt relaxed for the first time in a week of bad days.

Doc finished writing the wire messages for Wagner in Chicago. "I'll get these out at once. Sign the front of the report under my name."

Raider took a few seconds to slowly scribe his monicker. "I'll take this stuff down, Weatherbee. I'm goin' out anyway."

Doc had a puzzled expression on his countenance. "You? Volunteering to do something you loathe as much as paperwork? Are you daft?"

Raider shrugged, trying to look nonchalant. "Aw, hell, Doc, you're always pickin' up the heavy end of the bookwork. I just thought I'd spell you for a change."

Doc leaned back and poured himself a shot of the rye. He threw it down and sighed. "I'm too tired to argue with you, Raider. I appreciate the effort. Get out of here."

Raider bolted before his partner could come up with something else to detain him. He hurried out of the hotel, heading straight for the Western Union office. After determining that there were no messages for him or Doc, he gave the dispatches to the key operator. He asked as to the whereabouts of the post office but opted for a slight detour before he visited the postmaster.

Leaning against a counter at the telegraph office, Raider leafed through the report his partner had written. He took a deep breath and removed the last page, where Doc had been too hard on himself. That had to go.

"Ain't no reason to be bushwhackin' yourself, Weatherbee."

He wadded up the last page and threw it into a spittoon against the wall. Using a black ink-quill, he doctored the bottom of the new last page. When the sentence was right (a task that kept Raider busy for five minutes) he delivered the report to the postmaster, stressing in a short manner the importance of the document.

The postal man did not even charge him when he learned that Raider had been responsible for the demise of Ceron Lee. "He was a bad one, Mr. Pinkerton. I can tell you that. Glad his kind is gone around here."

Raider scoffed at the thin-faced clerk. "Plenty more where he came from, mister. Just be glad you got somebody to protect you from his kind. Time was, in these parts, criminals just took what they damn well wanted."

The clerk nodded. "Just be thankful them days is behind us."

"Are they, pardner? Are they really?"

Raider turned and walked out, leaving the postmaster to scratch his chin. As far as the big man from Arkansas could see, there wasn't a hell of a lot you could do about the evil inside a man. Wickedness could just plain take over a body. As an agent of the law, you were left with knowing that a bad soul would almost drive itself into a corner. Everything else was up in the air, unknowable. You just tried to stop evil and collect your pay, even if you figured it would never go away.

Raider stopped in the street, gazing up at the banners of two saloons that had opened for the day. He'd go to the one that had the earliest stakes game, unless of course it was faro, which Raider detested. The business with Ceron Lee had been bad luck, not Doc's carelessness. And Raider was ready to change his luck around.

He pushed through the swinging doors of the Double Dollar, glancing toward the round table where a slick-looking man shuffled a deck of cards.

Raider tipped back his Stetson. "Poker?"

The gambler nodded and gave him the high sign. But the big man from Arkansas never sat down at the table. Instead, he turned his eyes to the right, focusing on the source of a burst of derisive laughter. Two mangy men leaned against the bar, their hands resting over their six-shooters.

Raider's black eyes narrowed. "You boys wantin' to play some cards?"

A man in a buckskinned coat moved away from the bar. "Hear that? He don't recognize us."

The second man wore a bloodstained duster. "I reckon he roughs up so many people that he don't have time to remember their faces."

The gambler slipped quietly away from the table to hide in a back room.

Raider's hand dropped to his side, hovering over the Colt. He took a long look at the buckskinned man, waiting for him to move. The man's posture seemed familiar, but Raider could not place the features of his face.

The buckskinned man grinned at the big Pinkerton. "Last time I seen you, you had me by surprise, big 'un. Now we's face to face."

The duster man held up a bandaged hand. "You shot me pretty good, boy. I'm thinkin' it's time for me to oblige you."

Raider remembered now. "Cherokee Bend."

"That's right." said the man in buckskins. "And my name's Milo. And I'm gonna pull on you now, boy, and settle up the score."

Raider took a deep breath. "Boys, it's been a long trail. Now, you was both on the wrong end of the buffalo back there at the Bend. So let's not git our bridles on ass-backwards."

Milo grinned. "Hear that? He's turned weasel on us. Wants to slide in and hole up somewhere."

"Reckon he's scared of two of us."

Raider clenched his teeth. "You shouldna said that, boy."

Milo bristled. "You mighta shot up his hand, but he can still pull on you, big 'un. So can I."

Raider spread his feet to a comfortable stance. "It ain't whether or not I kill one of you or both of you, Milo. You see, it's more like, which one of you do I kill first. And even if you get a slug into me, I can still kill both of you before I fall."

The duster man licked his lips. "You know somethin', Milo, he's right."

"Shut up."

Raider's black eyes had glazed over. He stared at the man in the buckskin coat, waiting for the first sign of movement.

The duster man backed away, holding his hands in the air. He didn't want any more bandages, much less a shroud and a wooden coffin.

"Milo, you take him if you want—"

"Chicken shit! Git on out of here."

Raider held his stance. "Your friend has smarts, Milo. Now, what's it gonna be? You gonna let me play some poker, or are we gonna make it a real tough day for ever'body else?"

Milo's face was bright red. He scowled at Raider and then turned back toward the bar. The big man wheeled in the direction of the gaming table, keeping his hand over the butt of his .45. When he heard the rustling of the man's buckskins, he completed a circle, filling his hand with the Peacemaker.

Milo did not disappoint him.

As soon as Raider had turned, the bully of a man went for the Buntline on his hip. It was halfway out of the holster when the Peacemaker exploded in Raider's hand. A hunk of lead ripped an air hole in the man's chest. He staggered forward, gasping for wind, lifting the Buntline the rest of the way. Raider fanned the Colt, directing two bursts toward the man's gun hand. The Buntline fell to the floor, followed by the man who had been wielding it.

The duster man moved over the body of his dead friend. "You kilt him. You done kilt Milo."

"Tell me he wasn't asking for it."

The man's eyes lifted toward Raider. "You Pinkerton son of a bitch."

"Don't try it, boy."

But he tried it anyway. The duster man stood up, reaching for his pistol. Raider was going to wing him again, figuring he didn't have to kill him. But an explosion behind him precluded any attempt to prevent a double funeral.

The duster man's chest erupted in a flow of red.

Raider wheeled with his Colt to see the gambler standing next to the table holding a smoking scattergun. When the gambler saw the barrel of the .45, he dropped the shotgun and held up his hands. Raider exhaled and holstered the Peacemaker.

"You didn't have to kill him, partner."

The gambler was trembling. "He looked like he was going

to shoot you. Besides, we don't take to his kind in these parts anymore."

Raider scoffed. "Yeah, this town is gettin' to be a regular ladies' quiltin' party. How long you think we got till the law gits here?"

The gambler looked puzzled. "I don't know. Why?"

Raider strode to the table and took a chair. "Maybe we got time for a couple hands o' blackjack."

The dealer moved slowly toward his chair. "You want to play cards after you killed those two men?"

"After *we* killed them," Raider corrected. "Besides, I come in here to play cards. You want to deal me?"

The dealer sat down opposite the big man. "How can you think of cards after you—"

Raider leaned over the table. "Look, boy, them two was tryin' to kill me. Now if I let myself think about it, I'd be locked up in some place where they take crazy people, savvy? So I don't think about it any more'n I have to. Spin them cards, hombre. I'm bettin' five dollars."

He put a script note on the table.

The gambler shuffled the deck with trembling hands. "I thought you wanted to play poker."

Raider shrugged. "I reckon I changed my mind."

Killing a man could change a lot of things.

Raider's cards came good. Twenty on the first round, beating the dealer's nineteen. He let his bet ride and drew blackjack. Before he knew it there was twenty-five dollars in front of him. He let it ride one more time.

His cards fell—two sevens. The dealer showed a queen. Raider rubbed his chin, trying not to look back at the two corpses on the floor.

"You want me to hit you, cowboy?"

The marshal burst in through the swinging doors, his gun drawn. "I heared shootin' over here. What the . . ." He looked down at the two men at the gaming table.

"Stay," Raider said.

The dealer cringed. He flipped over his down card, a three of spades. He had to hit anything under eighteen.

The marshal started toward the table. "I'm askin' who done this to these two men?"

The dealer turned another queen, busting out with twenty-three.

Raider dragged his money—a hundred dollars—with the marshal looking over his shoulder. "Them boys was askin' for it, marshal."

"That's right," the gambler rejoined.

Raider dropped his winnings into his hat. "See, we had some trouble with these two when we was bringin' back Ceron Lee."

The marshal's eyes registered the big man's appearance. "Yes, I thought that was you, Mr. Raider." He looked at the bodies again. "So they pulled on you first, is that it?"

Raider nodded. "This gent was nice enough to back me up with a scattergun. Course, I coulda taken 'em both anyway."

"Of course," the marshal replied.

The gambler looked nervously at Raider. "You want me to deal you another hand, cowboy?"

Raider knew he wanted to get back that hundred dollars, but the big man was not obliging. "No, sir, but I might catch you later in the evenin'."

The marshal walked to the swinging doors and shouted for someone to go for the undertaker. When he turned back toward Raider, he was shaking his head. "Boy, you Pinks can sure scare up a bunch of trouble in a hurry. What'd you say these boys had agin you?"

Raider rose from his chair. "Not much, partner. We just had a little misunderstandin' that they took too serious. I tried to tell 'em to leave it be, but they wasn't havin' it."

The marshal nodded. "Bad eggs, I can tell you. Lucky you got to 'em before me."

Raider locked eyes with the lawman. "Lucky for who, Marshal?"

"Lucky for me, cowboy. I ain't as fast as I used to be."

Raider smirked. "No, but at least you're honest." He looked down at the bodies for the last time. "Any problems gonna come out of this for me?"

"No," the marshal replied. "Just gonna plant 'em. If we find any evidence of kin, there'll be a letter goin' out from the city and the state. Probably won't find a thing."

Raider looked away. "Probably not. I'll be at the hotel if you need me, Marshal."

He started for the swinging doors.

"Cowboy."

"Yeah?'

"Your partner was lookin' for you a while back. He said if I saw you to tell you to come right away. Said it was important."

"Damn."

"Something wrong?"

Raider just grunted and pushed through the swinging doors. If Doc was looking for him, it had to be something bad. He felt the weight of the money in his hat. His luck was flipping back and forth. But then when he thought about it, he realized that it had never been any other way. There wasn't really anything a man could to alter Fortune's turning wheel. You just had to take the numbers that came up, even when they weren't the right ones.

CHAPTER FOUR

"To hell with that!" Raider cried.

The big man stood up, pacing back and forth in front of Doc Weatherbee. His boots scruffed on the carpet of the hotel room floor. Complications had set in, promising to interfere with Raider's nighttime plans for drinking, gambling, and brothel jumping. Doc's news wasn't as bad as he had figured, it was just bothersome.

Raider's voice sounded weak. "A party, Doc? A fancy shindig with a lot of uppity people? You expect me to waltz into somethin' like that? I'd look like a' Injun at a Baptist social."

The man from Boston shrugged. He was obviously enjoying his partner's consternation. "We're going to be honored for the capture of Ceron Lee. The Citizens' Committee will bestow their highest award on us. A medal, I believe. Lee raped the daughter of the committee's chairman, not the mayor's daughter as we were led to believe."

Raider felt sick to his stomach. "How come they'd throw a shee-bang for me and you? Ain't it a lot of trouble for nothin'?"

"Well, I must confess that the entire affair is not in our honor. It seems the town of San Antonio and the state of Texas are involved in some sort of transaction concerning a piece of land nearby."

Raider scowled out the window. "Sounds complicated. Hell, they wouldn't miss a couple of no-accounts like us."

Doc looked indignant. "I do hope you are speaking of yourself. I'll have you know that—"

"Yeah, yeah, let's don't start up nothin' else. This dance has got me plenty spooked. I don't like dressin' up in some monkey suit and rubbin' against a bunch of dandified citizens."

Doc was determined to talk Raider into going. He had a morbid desire to see Raider bound by the confines of civilized society. He wondered how his partner would react to the pressure of manners and decorum.

"Raider, imagine that this will be like an old Arkansas square dance. We won't even be noticed until we receive our medals. Then I'll just make a short speech—"

"And put ever'body to sleep." Raider shook his head. "I don't know, Doc. You say they're gonna give us medals?"

"A big shiny one."

Raider rubbed his chin, peering out into the street. "I ain't never got a medal before."

Doc saw his partner swaying a little. "Of course, San Antonio's more pulchritudinous females will no doubt be impressed by our heroic exploits. Avenging the name of virtue, as it were."

Raider's brow fretted. "What?"

"The women will swoon."

Raider looked doubtful. "Probably be a bunch of proper ladies. I mean, you know me, Doc, I'm used to a different kinda girl. And I might feel funny with them fancy ladies. You know, sort of like a dog with no teeth gettin' loose in the smokehouse."

"At any rate, this *shindig* is tonight."

"Tonight! Hell, I was gonna—"

Doc stood up himself. "Of course, you can leave after we receive our commendations. You'd be all dressed and ready for a night on the town. And there will be quite a few ladies present at the ceremony. It would be a good gesture on behalf of the agency."

"Medals and women, huh?" A sly, almost canine smile spread over Raider's rough-hewn countenance. "You know,

Texas is awful close to Arkansas. This thing might just be like a down-home square dance."

Doc nodded, trying not to grin. "I'll suggest a tailor who can have you outfitted by tonight. By the way, do you have the receipts from the telegraph and the post offices?"

Raider hesitated before handing the receipts to his partner. Doc saw the look in the big man's black eyes. Sometimes he just knew when Raider was hiding something.

"We've been in San Antonio for two hours, Raider. Have you gotten into trouble already?"

Raider hung his head. He could tell Doc about killing the two men. He was really worried about keeping the doctored report a secret.

He looked up again. "See, Doc, I kinda ran into them two boys that was givin' you such a hard time in Cherokee Bend."

Doc grimaced his disapproval. "And you *kinda* had a fracas with them?"

Raider glanced away. "I kinda kilt one of them."

"And the other?"

Raider smiled weakly. "The gambler kilt him with a scattergun."

Doc threw up his hands. "Now there's a gambler in it."

"Hell, Weatherbee, they was askin' for it. Just a couple of saddle tramps with chips on their shoulders."

"Say no more," replied the man from Boston. "We must tell the marshal at once."

"The marshal knows all about it."

"And?"

Raider shrugged. "He didn't seem too worried about it either way. Seems they're dead set on tryin' to clean up San Antone."

Doc sighed, thinking he didn't want to write another report. "Then unless we hear about it later, you never told me. Do you understand? It never happened."

Raider eased back toward the door. "Thanks, Doc. And look, if I don't see you tonight, just—"

"No! You come to the party or we spend the rest of the day detailing your escapade in a directive to the home office."

Raider frowned. "That's bullshit, Doc. You can't blackmail me into comin' to that hoedown."

Doc scribbled something on a piece of paper. "Go to this address. Tell the man there that you want to be outfitted in formal evening attire. Charge the entire thing to my name. I'll take care of the tailor this afternoon when I call for my new suit."

Raider was fuming as he took the address from Doc's outstretched hand. He considered whaling the tar out of his partner, but he finally decided to just go along with it. Besides, he'd look good with a medal fixed on his chest. It was about time that he got a little credit for his expertise.

He'd just keep his mouth shut and smile at the ladies. When he had the medal, he'd slip out for a night in San Antonio. As long as he acted like a Southern gentleman, nothing could really go wrong. Nothing at all.

The official ceremonies were held in a huge opera house in the center of town. Ten rows of well-dressed citizens shifted in green velvet seats, staring up at the four men who stood downstage in front of a velvet curtain of the same color. Doc and Raider, clad in fancy suits, stood next to Freemont Biddle, head of the Citizens' Committee, and Hardy Tabor, a representative from the governor's office. The state and city were involved in a transaction in which the state was taking over a rather famous piece of land within the town limits. Doc and Raider were being honored almost as an afterthought.

Biddle, a waddling duck of a man, stepped forward to address the two hundred members of the audience. "Good evening, my friends." His voice was deep and resonant in the acoustics of the opera house. "As you know, we have three honored guests here tonight."

He stepped back and gestured toward Tabor, who was a slender, nattily dressed man of forty. "This gentleman is Hardy Tabor, who as you know is an aide to the governor of this great state."

A small offering of handclaps greeted the politician.

Biddle looked at the two detectives. "And these two men are agents of Allan Pinkerton himself. They did this town and this state a service by bringing to justice a thorn in the side of lawful citizens from here to Austin. On behalf of San Antonio and the State of Texas, I hereby award the Citizens' Medal to

Mr. Doc Weatherbee and his partner Mr. Raider."

The crowd erupted with applause. They stood up, giving Doc and Raider a standing ovation. The big man from Arkansas looked dazed as Biddle handed him the medal. Doc also seemed to lose his composure. His face was blank.

When Biddle had bestowed the commendations, he raised his hands to quiet the audience. "Now, now, they aren't running for mayor . . . yet."

Laughter from San Antonio's elite.

Biddle continued in his smooth delivery. "The sooner we dispense with the preliminaries, the sooner we get to the dance." More laughter. "I believe Mr. Tabor has a few words to say."

There was no applause as the slender gentleman stepped forward. "Thank you, Mr. Biddle. I simply want to say that the governor is very pleased with the impending purchase of the Mission of San Antonio de Valero, which you fine people know as the Alamo."

The Texans applauded heartily at the mention of their symbol of freedom.

Tabor smiled, waiting for the cheers to subside. "I can tell you this much. The state has big plans for this piece of land. I'm here to assure you that the Alamo will remain a part of our history as long as there's a free man on Texas ground."

More patriotic cheers and applause. Raider thought it was going to go on forever. He expected Doc to join in the speechifying, adding to the sentimental claptrap. But the man from Boston did not get to speak at all.

Instead, Hardy Tabor gestured upstage, toward the green curtain. "Ladies and gentlemen, the eyes of Texas are upon you."

The velvet curtain rolled up to reveal a small orchestra that broke into glorious song. The rest of the stage had been set up with long tables of food and drink. Doc and Raider were almost trampled in the stampede of citizens that flocked onstage for the banquet.

The big man from Arkansas sidestepped the well-wishers, tugging at his starched collar. "Damn glad this deal is over. Now I can git the hell out of this place."

Doc stopped him. "Not so soon. The citizens expect you to

mingle about. By all means, stay for a while. Pin on your medal and make the best of it."

"Aw hell, Doc."

Raider looked down at the case that held his commendation. He opened the box only to find that the medal did not look that impressive. He had done dirtier jobs for which he had received nothing but a hard time from the home office. He slipped the case into the pocket of his black suitcoat.

"Listen up, Doc, I'll see you back at the hotel."

He started to turn away, but a hand caught his arm.

"Doc, I don't want to—"

"Why, hello there, cowboy."

The big man peered down into a pair of devastating green eyes. The woman was older than he, but with her thick dark ringlets of hair and ridiculously low-cut dress, she presented an immediate attraction for any trail-weary saddle man. Raider tried not to focus on the shadow of her immense, sparsely covered bosom. He wasn't doing a very good job of being subtle, however.

"Doc, I think you better..."

But his partner was gone into the crowd, milling in to talk politics with the other cigar-wielding gentlemen.

The woman slipped her hand through Raider's arm, sidling closer to him. He began to sweat, fearing the temptations aroused by the scent of her perfume. He couldn't resist staring at her breasts.

The green-eyed woman made it rougher on him by acting as if they had been friends for years. "They call you Raider, don't they?"

He nodded nervously. "That they do, ma'am."

"Please, call me Abigail. Abigail Biddle."

Raider gawked at her. "Are you Mr. Biddle's wife?"

She laughed gaily. "No, Freemont is my brother. I'm widowed, you see. My husband died of cholera last year. I told him not to go on that hunting trip, but he wouldn't listen to me. He never was the tough sort—not like you, anyway."

He smiled weakly. "I thought you was too pretty to be a spinster."

She raised a thin eyebrow. "Thank you. I took back my maiden name because it was better known in these parts. That caused a scandal, I can tell you. You'd be surprised at the scandals in this town."

Raider felt like everyone was watching them. "Yeah, I reckon. I ain't really lookin' to start up another one."

She ignored his cautious tone. "If I weren't a widow, I could never get away with wearing a dress like this." She did a little turn for him, offering a busty pose. "Do you like it? It came all the way from France. I had to wait three months."

Raider nodded, trying to swallow. An involuntary stiffness had tightened the fabric of his suit pants. Her skin was so soft and smooth. She was a pampered lady, the kind he never got to . . . he tried to put the thoughts out of his mind. She was a very fancy lady—and her brother had given him the medal.

Abigail leaned closer to his ear, brushing his arm with her magnificent chest. "I hear you're the one who killed that Ceron Lee."

Raider shrugged, feeling the perspiration on his forehead. "Well, I reckon I had some part in it, but he was really kicked in the head by my partner's ornery mule."

Abigail did not seem to hear him. "You are a brave man. My niece was the one he supposedly raped."

Raider tried to look concerned. "Sorry to hear that."

"Ha." She practically brushed his ear with her lips. "But I can tell you right now that she was carrying on with that varmint of her own free will. That little tramp was bad from the day she was born. My brother started the rape story to cover up the whole sordid mess."

Raider was on fire inside his suit. He had to get away from her. If he got out of line, Doc would never let him hear the end of it.

Abigail reached into his coat pocket. "Can I see your medal?"

Raider did not protest.

"Oh, it's so pretty. But only bronze. That cheap brother of mine could have paid for gold, but he's as tight as a drum."

Raider shrugged, wiping his forehead. "I'm obliged for what he gave me."

"You're sweating. Here, let me."

Her unblemished hand raised a handkerchief to his face.

Raider thought he was going to faint as she dabbed the moisture from his brow. When she lifted her arm, he peered directly into the canyon of her bosom.

He pulled back a little. "That's all right, Miss Biddle."

"Call me Abby."

Raider tried to think of some polite way to ditch her. If he hung around much longer, he might make an ass of himself. You never knew where you stood with proper women. They could be treating you just fine, and then—*boom*—they wouldn't throw water on you if you caught fire.

"I just need me a cold drink, Abby. Maybe I can get somethin' for you."

"Why, yes, I could use some refreshment."

Raider patted her hand. "Stay right here. I'll be back in just a minute."

"What about your medal?"

"Hang on to it," he replied, starting away from her.

The image of her bosom would not leave his mind as he fought his way through the crowd. He came face to face with Doc as he neared the table where a huge punch bowl rested. The man from Boston smiled devilishly.

"Having a good time, Raider?"

The big man scowled. "I'm gettin' the hell out of here while I still have my head screwed on."

"But . . ."

"No buts, Doc. I'm gone."

He started for the side exit, thinking that Abigail would stay put. Leaving the medal with her had been a good touch. If she thought he was coming back, she wouldn't look for him. Or so he thought.

As he neared the side door, a buxom figure blocked his path. "Going somewhere, Mr. Raider?"

"Er, just goin' out for some air, Miss Biddle."

She smiled. "I thought you were going to call me Abigail." She slid closer to him. "Why were you going to leave me, cowboy? Don't you like the way I look?"

Raider's mouth was dry. "I wasn't leavin', like I told you, I was just goin' outside for a fresh breath."

"I'm too quick for you." She kissed his cheek. "I do hope

you aren't scared of me, cowboy."

His eyes focused on her breasts again. "No, I ain't. I mean, why would I leave with you holdin' that medal for me?"

She popped open the case and examined the award again. "I can't imagine this little nothing being important to a man like you." Her eyes came up to meet his. "How would it look on me?"

"Try it."

She stepped back, but instead of pinning the medal on her dress, she placed it in the cleft between her pallid globes of bouncing flesh. Her bosom swelled as she took a deep breath. Raider detected the slight trembling on her lips.

"How do you like it, cowboy?"

Raider shook his head. "You're a handsome woman, Abby. But I ain't the kind of man you want to—"

Her finger pressed against his mustache. "Shh." She looked over his shoulder, checking the other party guests. "Good, no one has seen us."

Raider's knees felt weak. "Abby, I don't think it's a good idea for us to be back here without—"

She pulled down his face, kissing him for a long time, all tongue and teeth. Her hand closed on the rigid lump between his thighs. Raider gulped for air, knowing that he was defeated. Cupping both of her breasts in his rough hands, he started to return the kiss.

She broke away quickly. "Not here."

"Where?"

"Come on, I want to give you a tour of the theater."

Raider did not protest as she took his hand and guided him into the backstage shadows.

Doc Weatherbee stood among the party guests, firing up the end of a fresh cheroot, listening to the governor's aide, Hardy Tabor.

"Yes, Weatherbee, we're on our way to being the finest state in the Union. Not just the biggest, mind you, but the best. Cattle, railroads, cotton. You name it and Texas has got it."

Doc nodded, slipping the silver matchbox into his coat

pocket. "Mr. Tabor, what does the state plan to do with the Alamo property?"

The slender gentleman smiled his noncommittal politician's smirk. "We aren't exactly certain as of yet. But I'm sure we'll think of something."

The man from Boston exhaled a billow of smoke. "I'm sure you will."

Tabor looked awfully content with himself. Doc made excuses, trying to get away. He sauntered toward another group of distinguished gentlemen but found that the governor's aide was right behind him. Again Tabor launched into a patriotic dialogue that drew complacent smiles from the wide-girthed local gentry.

"Yes, gentlemen, the Mexicans gave us a fight at the Alamo, but I daresay the days of trouble are over. The brave are dead and buried, and the state plans to do right by them and by this great city."

Doc stopped listening. He cast his eyes over the bobbing heads of the party guests, looking for Raider, but he didn't see the big man's figure in the crowd. Doc wondered if his partner felt Tabor's compulsion to do right by the fine people of San Antonio. He found himself hoping that Raider had fled the gathering for a soiree more suited to his brutish tastes.

Abigail Biddle was full of surprises. She led Raider through the dim wings of the theater, taking him deeper into the backstage darkness. Finally she stopped and asked Raider if he had a match. The big man had one sulphur-tipped stick in his pocket, a leftover from the two matches Doc had given him to melt his boot polish.

Abigail used the match to light a single candle. When the circle of flame burned evenly, Raider saw that they were standing at the door of some kind of dressing room. There were mirrors and costumes on the wall.

He laughed. "Are we gonna put on some kind of show, Abby?"

She turned to smile at him. "That depends on you, cowboy. Are you ready to perform?"

Raider responded by cupping her breasts and lowering his

lips to hers. For a minute he thought she was going to suck out his tongue. But she broke away finally, breathless from the kiss.

"No," she said. "This place is to obvious. Someone might come looking for us."

Raider squinted at her. He wasn't ready for the tease and then the letdown. His male urgency needed to be satisfied.

"Abby, it ain't right to lead a fella on and then drop him while his Johnson is still—"

Again she put a finger to his lips. "I'm as ready as you are, Raider. We just have to make a few adjustments."

While Raider considered the meaning of "adjustments," Abigail Biddle moved closer to the wall of the dressing room. She disconnected a latch and pulled open a sliding door. Raider smiled and picked up the candle, following her into a narrow recess behind the door.

"The dressing rooms are joined by this closet," said Abby. "Both doors can be locked from the inside. We can get out, but nobody can get in."

Raider lifted the candle. "Kinda small, ain't it?"

Her hand massaged his crotch again. "It will suit us. Raider, you have to promise me that you won't tell anyone about this. I have a reputation as it is. I don't know what came over me when I saw you up on that platform. I just knew I wanted you anyway I could have you. Have you ever felt that way about someone?"

Raider shrugged. "Well, there was this little filly down in Brownsville."

"A woman?"

"More like a horse. She was fine and ready to run."

Abby moved closer to him, running her hands over his chest. "Why don't we take off your coat? I'd like to see you —oh, what's this?"

Her hands had found the derringer inside Raider's coat pocket.

He pushed her away for a moment. "I couldn't bring my six-gun, so I packed somethin' a little smaller."

She kissed him for a long time. Raider ran his hands over her backside, but felt only layers of lace and velvet. He had to get her out of the dress so he could caress her soft skin. His entire body ached for her.

"Let me see what I can do with these buttons."

"No," she replied softly. "I'll undress you first. Blow out the candle, if you don't mind."

Raider lifted the candle toward a narrow shelf on the wall of the enclosure. "I want light, Abby. I want to see you, to see how beautiful you are. Ugly has to hide in the dark, and you sure ain't that."

"My God, you do know how to talk to a woman."

Her hands went to work, disrobing the tall cowboy. She hung his coat and shirt on hooks that protruded from the wall. Raider hesitated when she went for the buttons of his pants.

"We can just pull 'em down," he said. "I don't want to take off my boots. You understand me? We might have to get out of here quick-like."

Abby rubbed his hairy chest, kissing his nipples. "I just want you, and I don't care how I get it."

Again she went to work on his pants, slowly unbuttoning the fly, raising her green eyes to watch his reaction. When his penis broke free, a gasp escaped from her lips. She mused for a moment before she summoned the courage to touch Raider's erect member.

"You still want it, Abby?"

"More than ever, cowboy." She looked up into his face. "Have you been with many women?"

"My share."

Raider wondered if all society women liked to talk at the exact moment when conversation was the last thing on his mind.

She continued playing with him. "I'll bet you've had every girl west of the Mississippi."

Raider just laughed.

Then she did something that really seemed odd to the big man. She unhitched her dress, freeing her breasts from the cumbersome garment. Raider reached for her nipples, but she knelt down in front of him.

"Have you done disgusting things with women, cowboy?"

"Honey, I don't know what you're—"

She pushed her breasts together, holding his cock between them. "How does that feel?"

"Fine, Abby, just fine."

His prick rolled around in the crack of her bosom for a while. Then she looked up at him with those lustful green eyes. "I just love French things. Did you ever do French things with women?"

"Abby, if you'd just—"

"I'm going to do French things to you, cowboy."

And she did, taking the head of his prick between her lips. Her awkward mouthing brought a dribble of sour liquid from the end of Raider's cock. She drew back, spitting at the taste.

"I've never done that before," she said. "Did I do it right?"

"Just damned fine."

She stood up to kiss him, but Raider avoided her mouth. He lowered his lips to her huge breasts, sucking on the pink nipples that were as big as silver dollars. Abby's fingers gripped his dark hair. Her breath had become heavy and erratic.

Raider's hands fought with the layers of petticoats beneath her velvet dress. He could not find a path to her crotch. Abby tried to help him by lifting the crinoline over her hips, but the crotch proved to be too thick. Raider gave a grunt of exasperation.

"You wearin' ever'thing you own, woman?"

Abby gripped his penis tightly. "I want that thing inside me. Here, let me lie down."

She stretched out on the floor, spreading her legs. Raider knelt down, still looking for his prize in the billows of cloth. He thought his testicles were going to explode if he didn't release his manly burden.

Abby offered a throaty chortle. "Keep at it, cowboy. A man has to be persistent. If you'd just . . . what are you doing?"

Raider had stuck his head underneath her dress. He fought his way through the petticoats, ripping away the fabric with his hands and teeth. Finally he was in the vicinity of his destination. He tore away a piece of lace to feel the warmth of Abby's femininity.

"Are you going to do French things to me, cowboy?"

Raider figured it didn't matter much, since he had already come so far. Her body twitched when he touched his lips to the crest of her cunt. Thick thighs tightened against his cheeks, almost suffocating him. He had to withdraw from beneath her skirts to find fresh air.

"Get on top of me," she beckoned.

Raider obliged her, settling into the warmth between her legs. She kissed her own juices from his lips as he attempted an awkward, prodding entry. His cock was having a difficult time finding its mark. Abby pulled up her undergarments and seized his manhood. He felt her wetness on the head of his prick.

"Go in hard," she whispered. "All the way."

"Yes, ma'am," he replied, thinking that he should always be polite to society ladies.

Abby cried out when he entered her. She spread her legs wider, propping her feet against the walls of the closet. Her breasts jiggled with each powerful thrust of the big man's hips.

"Oh God," she moaned. "It's never felt like this. Never."

Sometimes women just had to talk while they were doing it.

Raider did not let her dialogue distract him. He slowed for a while, taking it in and out of her, lowering his mouth to her nipples, kissing and biting with tenderness. Abby's body stiffened with her first climax. He drove his cock deep inside her and left it there for a few moments.

"You're damned well tickling my fancy," she whispered.

Raider was gearing up for his own release when she grabbed his shoulders.

"Somethin' wrong, Abby?"

"No." She drew air through her closed lips. "I just want to do nasty things with you. Let's do something nasty."

Raider frowned a little. "Like what?"

"Surprise me."

He drew his cock out of her. "All right, if that's what you want."

Her green eyes were wide with anticipation. A trembling overtook her thick lower lip. The big man touched her cheek.

"You sure you want it?"

"Yes. Yes."

"All right. Turn it around. Get down on all fours. You understand."

She quickly assumed the animalistic posture. "I never did this with my husband. Never."

"He might not have gone huntin' if you had," Raider replied.

With her backside to him, he peeled back the layers of cloth. Her white ass offered him a vertical smile. Raider gave her plump cheeks a little smack with the flat of his hand, prompting a moan from Abby's lips.

"I didn't hurt you, did I?" Raider asked.

She shook her head. "Do it again. Harder."

He popped her butt again, but he held back. Hurting women wasn't big on Raider's list of lustful activity. His hand smoothed the pink mounds of her backside, working down the crack to the moist beard between her thighs.

"Let's take it real easy, honey."

"Just put it inside me. And don't shoot in there. Pull it out when you—ooh!"

He rested his cock against her crevice. Abby moved her backside, trying to accommodate his entry. Raider grabbed her hips and sunk his cock to the hilt. She moaned and then rocked backward. Raider reached forward to cup her hanging breasts as he humped her.

"That's so deep," she groaned. "Don't stop. Don't stop."

Their bodies shook in unison. Raider drove his hips to the point of exhaustion, but he couldn't find his release. Abby seemed to be enjoying herself, however. Three times he felt her tense up, quivering as if some sort of fever had gripped her buxom frame.

"You do me right, cowboy."

"Let's get back the way we was," Raider said. "I want to climb on top of you again."

Abigail obliged him in a hurry. She spread out, wriggling on her back. Raider slipped into the notch of her cunt, spearing her again with his aching cock.

"Pull it out when you do," she whispered.

She tried to move with him when he started up again. But

Raider was too fast. He bounced between her thighs, causing her face to contort in a desperate expression of delight and agony. She could only lie there and submit to his thrusts, taking her own pleasure in the same orgasmic instant.

Raider thought he was never going to climax. He quit trying to hold back, concentrating on his lusty efforts to release. Abby had put her hand over her mouth, whimpering and shaking her head back and forth.

"Please, cowboy. Please."

But Raider still didn't come.

He slowed for a moment, putting his face between her breasts. Abby traced the bumps of his spine, guiding her fingers toward the crack of his ass. Raider looked up when he felt her finger prodding his anus.

"What the hell are you—"

She sunk a finger into him, triggering an automatic release. Raider tried to pull out, but his cock was spewing. He managed to withdraw finally, depositing the remainder of his discharge on the curly hair of her pubic mound. She pulled out her finger.

He shook his head. "Where'd you learn that?"

She smiled wickedly. "My husband used to get drunk and want it. He couldn't do it up though, so I'd help him along a little bit."

Raider started to roll off her.

"No."

She wrapped her legs around his waist.

"Put it back inside me. Please."

He was half limp, but he still penetrated the soft folds of flesh. Abby sighed, holding him inside. The big man nuzzled her breasts, licking the erect buds of her nipples.

She smiled at him. "You ever thought about getting married, cowboy?"

"Sometimes," he replied. "But not very often."

She chortled. "Of course not. Men like you don't settle down, do they? Not even with women as rich as I am. My husband left me a bundle, you know."

Raider looked into her green eyes. "You sure you told him *not* to go on that hunting trip?"

"You know how men are," she replied. "If you tell them not to do something, they go right out and do it."

"Kinda like women, huh?"

She slapped him on the butt.

Raider just laughed.

Abby's tongue rolled outside her mouth, licking her lips. She decided to test her theory about males. "Don't you dare fuck me again, cowboy. You hear me? Don't you start up."

Raider probably would have proved her right. He was certainly in the position to do so. But just as he shifted his hips again, voices resounded outside the closet door. Both of them froze in the narrow enclosure. They listened for a moment, wondering what to do.

Then all hell broke loose, and Raider grappled to pull up his pants in the confusion.

CHAPTER FIVE

The commotion outside the costume closet began as two low, angry, growling voices. Then, above the whisper, a man cried out, "I'm not going to do it, and that's the final say!" The second party mumbled something indistinguishable, followed by scuffling and banging against the walls of the chamber.

At the first signs of the struggle, Raider leapt to his feet, hitching up his trousers. As he reached for the derringer in his coat pocket above, a lumpy weight thumped against the closet door. Raider wheeled with the small-caliber pistol in time to see the bloody knife blade protruding two inches through the soft wood of the door. The blade withdrew from the candlelight and the body crumpled to the floor.

Raider knew the unmistakable death chortle of a man drawing air through a hole in his throat. A goner for sure on the other side of the wall. The big man tried the door, but the dead man was wedged against it, jamming the aperture.

"The other one!" Abby said in a rasping whisper. "It connects to a room on the same hall."

Raider shushed her and slid through the second door into the darkness of an adjacent chamber. Lifting the derringer, he hugged the wall, moving into the corridor toward the source of the disturbance, hoping the knife man had not heard him. Easing into the threshold, he lowered the pistol at the dark figure that hovered over the fresh corpse. The killer seemed to be looking through the dead man's pockets.

"I think you done about enough meanness for one night, partner. Just hold her right there and . . . hey, boy, I'm talkin' to you."

In the backstage dimness, Raider wasn't sure that he *saw* what actually happened next. He *heard* the rustling of the man's garments and he *felt* the cracking of his knuckles when the foot kicked his gun hand. As both barrels of the pistol exploded, a shadowy, crouching man shape was perceptible in the brief flash.

Later the big man would say he had never known anyone to move so fast. He lunged toward the man shape only to wrap his arms around thin air. Breaking glass in front of him. The man had crashed through the window, sailing out into the shadows of the evening.

Raider moved to the sill and looked down. They were on the second floor. It was a long drop to the alley. He couldn't see the man, nor had he heard the dead-meat thudding of a body hitting the earth.

"Son of a bitch. Where'd he go?"

For a moment he thought he heard footfalls, but then Doc and the others rushed in behind him, carrying lanterns and talking in loud, excited voices. Raider realized that he wasn't wearing a shirt. He thought for a moment about Abby in the closet, but his eyes fell again on the body that was lying against the door.

He was an older man, with graying hair and wrinkles. He had been dressed up in a suit, undoubtedly one of the party guests. The hole in his neck emptied thick, warm streaks of blood onto his white shirt.

"Everyone back!" Doc cried.

San Antonio's elite were pushing and straining to get a gander at the new topic of gossip and conversation.

Doc pulled out his Pinkerton credentials and brandished them officially. "Please, go back to the stage. Allow the marshal to get through."

Raider slid next to a rack of costumes and found himself a white shirt that looked sort of sissy-like. Nevertheless, the big man employed the shirt to cover his bare chest. He couldn't quite get it buttoned, but it was better than having Doc asking a bunch of questions about his naked torso. He hoped Abigail was safely back with the crowd.

"Let us by, confound it!"

It was the voice of Freemont Biddle. He elbowed his way through the crowd, pushing into the room with the marshal and the state man, Hardy Tabor. Biddle gasped and turned ashen when he saw the body lying on the floor. The marshal shook his head and took a colder look. Hardy Tabor turned away holding his stomach.

The marshal looked at Raider. "This another one of your jobs, son?"

Raider scowled at the lawman. "I buried my daddy a long time ago, hombre."

The marshal's hand moved under his coat. "Just seems strange to find you ever'time I come up on a dead 'un."

Raider's body tilted toward the marshal, but Doc quickly stepped between them. "There's no need for hostilities, sir. If you will only hold your suspicions for a moment, I will help you clear up this entire matter. Mr. Tabor, will you close that door?"

The governor's aide obeyed Doc, still not looking at the body.

Biddle put a hand to his mouth and stifled his gagging. Raider thought maybe the old geezer was going to croak on them. He wondered what Freemont would do if he found out the big man had been tapping his sister.

"Mr. Weatherbee," Biddle said, "I want you to assume the lead in this matter. I give you total responsibility. I shall wire your superiors immediately. If you—"

"Now hold on," the marshal said, "I'm the chief law officer in this town. If anybody's gonna—"

Biddle glared at him. "Don't you understand who that is lying there on the floor?"

"I was hoping you'd tell us," Doc replied.

Biddle's eyes bulged. "His name is—was Hollis Morton. He's a respected citizen, a banker who helped build this town."

"He helped to build this entire state," Tabor said.

Doc turned toward the state man. "Did you know him?"

Tabor shook his head. "Not personally. But he was a supporter of the governor. One of those faceless men who seek no personal credit. He was content to remain in the background, but he was no less a Texan for it."

Doc glanced down at the body again. "Any ideas as to who might want him dead?"

Biddle shook his head. Tabor shrugged. The marshal had a baffled expression in his eyes.

Doc took a deep breath. "Then I shall endeavor to find out who killed him and why. Now, if everyone will remain still, I will have a look around the room to ascertain anything that might aid us in finding the killer."

The marshal chortled derisively. "What's to find out? He's been kilt in here with a knife."

Raider smirked at the lawman's ignorance of Doc's methods. "Hell, Marshal, when a bobcat leaves tracks in the snow, you don't rightly see him, but you know he's been there."

Doc looked up at his partner. "We'll start with what Raider knows."

The marshal eyed the big man suspiciously. "Yeah, what was you doin' in here so quick?"

Raider's eyes narrowed. "I spilled somethin' on my shirt. I was lookin' for a place to clean it off. I come in here and stepped into the closet there so nobody would see me with my shirt off."

"Why didn't you just change in here, just close this door?" The marshal had snapped the question like he was planning to catch Raider at something.

"Hell," the big man replied, "when I saw how big that closet was, I just went in. Figured I might find another shirt. And I did, if you'll see this one I got on."

The marshal decided to go to the adjoining chamber and check out the closet from the other side. Raider held his breath, praying that Abigail Biddle had made a clean getaway. When the marshal came back, he was holding the rest of Raider's suit.

"His shirt is stained all right," the marshal said. "Only it looks like rouge to me."

"Gimme that!" Raider snatched his belongings out of the marshal's hand.

Doc ignored the rouge stain. "When did you first hear or see any signs of a struggle, Raider?"

The big man laid it all out for his partner, how the body had blocked the door, the speed and agility of the murderer, the escape through the window. "Doc, how could he have gone out of there without getting killed on the ground?"

Biddle, Tabor, and the marshal were curious as well.

"I will explain, or attempt to explain that later," Doc replied. "Raider, did you get a good look at the assailant?"

"Not really. He seemed small, kinda. Only . . . he was crouchin' over the body when I come in. Like he was lookin' for somethin'."

Doc looked at the marshal. "Sir, I would like to have your permission to search the pockets of this gentleman. After all, you are the head of the constabulary in San Antonio, and our investigation should be carried out with the complete knowledge and cooperation of your office."

The marshal didn't understand the last part too well, but he gave Doc permission to search the remains of one Hollis Morton, banker.

The man from Boston bent down and carefully went through the pockets of the deceased. He brought a wallet out of the man's inside coat pocket. It bore several hundred dollars in cash and an image of the man's wife, also deceased according to Biddle. Morton also had a set of keys, some coins, a rabbit's foot, and two fine cigars.

Raider peered down at what death had left behind. "Hell, ain't much there worth filchin'. Why didn't he take the wallet?"

Doc turned over the wallet to the marshal. "I don't believe our man was looking for money." Doc flipped the key ring in his hand. The dead man had kept his keys on a thin loop of rawhide. Doc held up the ring for his partner to examine.

"Look here, Raider. The knot on this leather thong has been tied and untied recently. See there, where the old knot had been. As if Morton had added or eliminated a key from his chain."

Raider scratched his head, studying Doc. The gentleman

Pinkerton had that *look* in his blue eyes. He had grabbed a thread, and he wouldn't stop until he had unraveled the whole bolt of cloth.

Doc went back into the dead man's pockets. The blood was drying on Morton's chest. How could a mule-loving, Yankee-bred dandy have so much liver when it came to blood and guts?

"Ah-ha," he cried, "a hole in his coat pocket. If I can just rip it a little bigger . . ." Sound of tearing cloth. "There. Perhaps I will find what I'm looking for in the lining. What? I believe that's it."

He held it up for all of them to see.

"What is it?" asked Tabor.

Doc looked at his partner. "Tell him, Raider."

"Wells Fargo strongbox key," the big man replied.

Biddle mopped his forehead with a handkerchief. "But why would Hollis have taken that key off the leather thong?"

Doc raised his finger. "He obviously removed the key from the ring because he did not want the assailant to find it."

"That makes sense," Tabor replied. "But why the hole in his pocket?"

"Isn't it obvious?" Doc watched their faces until he realized it was not obvious to anyone but him. "The assailant was at the party tonight, gentlemen."

He gave them enough time to digest that and then moved on. "I believe that Morton saw the gentleman who murdered him. He untied the key ring and pushed the Wells Fargo key into the lining of his coat. Now, this tells us two things. One, that Morton was surprised by the mystery guest, and two, that he did not want this key to fall into the hands of the same man. There is something, somewhere in a Wells Fargo box that Mr. Morton did not want to surrender to his killer."

The marshal blew out a long wheeze. "Then let's get over to Morton's house and find that box."

"There are legal channels for that sort of thing, Marshal," Doc replied. "He might have family; they should be notified."

Biddle shoved the marshal toward the door. "Confound it, you overpaid, tin-starred . . . let the Pinkertons handle this."

Doc, playing the diplomat, said, "I will need the marshal's assistance while we search for other clues, Mr. Biddle."

"What else you lookin' for?" the marshal inquired.

Doc pointed to the window. "Aren't you the least bit curious as to why and how the murderer was able to escape through that window?"

The marshal scratched behind his ear. "Hey, you reckon his body is down there in the alley?"

Raider shook his head. "I didn't hear no thud."

"Well, maybe your ears is plugged up," the marshal said.

Before they could get into it, Doc bade them have a look. Biddle and Tabor remained behind to see to the body. There wouldn't be any problem getting the late Hollis Morton to the funeral parlor. The undertaker was in attendance at the party. Only he did not like to be called an undertaker. Around town, the man had been telling everyone that he was now a mortician. He had even made up a sign with his name on it. A regular pillar of the community. Raider didn't care what you called it, dead was dead, and the bonepicker put you six feet under. He supposed it didn't matter to the departed, however. Dead men weren't much for names. Not much at all.

In the alley, the marshal held the lantern while Doc and Raider searched the ground for signs of the killer. The earth was packed hard, rendering no tracks but providing a tough landing for anyone who had plummeted out of a window. Still, there was no evidence that anyone had hit the dirt hard enough to cause serious injury.

Raider shook his head. "That boy might've been able to fly, Doc."

"Doubtful," replied the man from Boston. "However, he could have been possessed of great strength and agility."

Raider tipped back his Stetson. "He was quick all right. And strong, too. Popped that gun out of my hand like it was nothin'."

Doc turned back to the lawman. "Marshal, could you hold that lantern a bit higher?"

The marshal complied. The opera house was bordered by a smaller structure—a warehouse, according to the marshal. The roof of the warehouse was only ten or twelve feet below the window of the dressing room.

Doc gazed upward, between the two buildings. "He could

have jumped onto the roof of the warehouse," Doc offered.

"That's a long way to fly," Raider said skeptically.

Doc nodded. "But look there, at the pole extending from the roof of the warehouse. A flagpole. Am I correct, Marshal?"

The lawman nodded, as if he was glad to be included in Doc's process of reasoning. "Sure is a flagpole. This used to be the front of the building before the opera house was built. Old Klag Moser flies it up there on the Fourth of July and any other holiday to do with the Union or the state of Texas. Don't even care about if anybody can see it or not."

Doc pointed to the window. "Now, let's say the man went out at a full clip, flew until he hit the flagpole, and slid down. He could then swing off the roof into the alley."

Raider scowled. "Shit, Doc, he'd have to be a monkey or somethin'."

Doc nodded. "A monkey or a trained acrobat. Marshal, is the circus in town, by any chance?"

"No siree."

"Hmm." Doc considered everything for a moment before he temporarily gave it up. "So much for now. Shall we indulge ourselves in a hasty reconnoiter of the alley area?"

The marshal squinted at Raider. "What'd he say?"

"We're gonna look around back here," the big man replied.

The marshal shook his head. "Danged me if you boys ain't a step or two ahead of my old noggin'."

"Aw, don't let it throw you, Marshal. Ol' Doc there is about two bricks too many on a load. I don't savvy about half of what he's sayin', but I can usually get the drift."

As they moved down the alley with the lantern, the marshal seemed to be considering something. "Raider, I'm sorry about all the mix-up in there when we was—"

"Forget it, marshal."

"No, what I'm sayin' is that you boys *should* be handlin' this instead of me. I can see that now."

Doc called to them from a few feet away. He was standing near the wall of the warehouse, looking down. "He landed here, all right."

The marshal's lantern revealed the slightest mark where the

toe of a boot had nudged the hard earth. The lawman shook his head again. "I'd never have seen that."

Doc looked up. "I wonder what's on the roof?"

Raider sighed. "I reckon you want me to go up there and find out."

Doc shrugged. "If you're willing."

Raider shinnied up a drainpipe, reaching back for the lantern when he was on the roof. He searched for a while until he found a scrap of paper. When he opened it up, he saw that it was covered with lines and scratches from a pen. It didn't look like much, but he went back down and showed it to Doc anyway. The man from Boston was puzzled as well.

"Looks like some kinda map," the marshal offered.

"Possibly," Doc replied. "Crude, of course. Look at this blob of ink here. And this looks like the letter T. Two lines going away from each other here a a forty-five-degree angle."

Raider sighed. "Well, we ain't got any way of knowin' that our man dropped this or not. Could be anything."

Doc slipped the paper into his pocket. "Yes, it could be. Shall we continue our search?"

But after another half hour, they were ready to quit. The marshal repeated his desire to let Doc and Raider handle the case. He would help, naturally, but as far as he could see, the two Pinkertons were out of his league. He left them in the alley, returning to the opera house to make sure the body had been properly removed.

When they were alone, Doc looked at his partner. "We haven't even had time to rest, and we're already onto another case."

Raider grunted. "Yeah, well, Wagner ain't said we could take it just yet. He might not want us gettin' mixed up in this local business."

Doc smiled accusingly at his partner. "Who was she, Raider?"

The big man squinted hatefully. "What?"

"The woman."

"Ain't been with no woman, Doc."

The man from Boston twisted the knife. "Shall we recall the rouge stain on your shirt?"

"Mind your own taters. Besides, ain't we got us a murder case now? Ain't you happy enough to go pokin' around in ever'body's damned bees-wax?"

Doc tipped his derby and followed after the marshal.

"Damned smarty pants!" Raider called.

The big man's stomach was churning, but he was not upset over Doc's accusations. Nor was he afraid that Freemont Biddle might find out about the steamy liaison in the costume closet. One thought kept going through Raider's mind—if he had gotten his pants on quicker, Hollis Morton might not have taken a knife in the throat. If he had been one instant faster . . . But a man could drive himself crazy thinking about *ifs*, and Raider had no intention of becoming a madman. He shook it off and followed his partner.

Hollis Morton had no relatives, no immediate family, no offspring from his marriage. When they called first thing the next morning at his residence, they were greeted by a Mexican housekeeper who spoke little English. Doc, Raider, and Freemont Biddle spent the better part of half an hour trying to convince the maid to allow them to enter. She refused to believe that Morton was dead, and only after an interpreter was summoned did she break down into tears at the inevitable truth.

When the housekeeper was comforted, Doc entered Morton's private study and spent the entire morning searching through the dead man's personal belongings. According to Biddle, Morton had retired several months earlier from his position at the First Bank of San Antonio. As far as Biddle knew, the old gentleman had been passing his days reading, fishing, and hunting. He had been perfectly content, and there was no reason to suspect that anyone would have wanted him dead.

Doc found no evidence in Morton's study to convince him otherwise. There was no strongbox for the Wells Fargo key, and no sign that Morton had anything to hide. The seventy-two-year-old banker appeared to have been a genial elder, the kind of man who spent a great deal of his time with the Good Book in one hand and a fishing pole in the other.

After four hours of shuffling through Morton's study, Doc

came up with one thing that might help them—a receipt from the Wells Fargo office.

Raider eyed the paper with skepticism. "You reckon they're gonna just turn over that strongbox to us?"

Doc shrugged. "Our status as Pinkerton agents might help. Of course, the usual legal channels are open if we—"

"Confound it," Biddle bellowed, "I want results, Weatherbee. We'll get that strongbox if we have to enlist the militia."

Biddle led them to the Wells Fargo office, where the clerk surrendered the strongbox without a single question.

Doc tried the key, turning it enough to know that it worked. He did not open the box, however, which brought a glare of consternation to the eyes of the Citizens' Committee chairman.

"Aren't you going to have a look, Weatherbee?"

Doc shook his head. "Not here, sir."

Biddle looked confused. "But why not?"

"A man was murdered, possibly over the contents of this box. When I open it, I want to be alone, or at least in private. If Morton was, as you say, an upstanding member of the community, then the evidence herein might go a long way toward sullying his reputation. Do you understand?"

Biddle turned a bright shade of red. "Are you saying that Hollis was involved in some wrongdoing?"

"He was killed, wasn't he?" Raider chimed in. "Me and Doc have seen a lot of men come down the chute. You never know what's swimmin' around inside somebody till you lay open the truth."

Suddenly Biddle's eyes shone with a political gleam. "Yes, I see. We should be careful in this. My word, I hope this doesn't have anything to do with the First Bank."

Doc hoisted the strongbox, which was light. No gold inside—at least not a large amount. Raider offered to help, but the man from Boston lugged the box by himself, heading for the hotel. Biddle followed them until Doc entered his room and closed the door.

"Perhaps I should send for someone to sit with him," Biddle offered.

Raider shrugged. "Listen, you got the best man for the job sittin' right in there with that strongbox."

"I wish I could be sure."

"Come on and have a snort with me, Freemont."

Biddle glanced sideways when the big man used his first name, but he still accepted Raider's invitation to have a shot of whiskey at the saloon. The older gentleman's disposition seemed to improve with the glow of the red-eye. He still kept looking back toward the hotel, as if he expected Doc to come bursting through the saloon doors with the answer to the mystery of Hollis Morton's untimely demise.

Raider knew better. "He ain't comin' right away, Freemont."

"What's that?" Biddle said, spinning around toward the big cowboy.

Raider snorted, throwing back a shot of whiskey. "Doc's about the smartest ol' boy I ever knew, not countin' some of the men we've come up against. Course, no matter how smart they was, Doc always seems to outsmart 'em some way or other."

Biddle emptied his glass in a quick gulp. "If he's so all-fired smart, why is he taking so long and being so—"

"He likes to study on somethin' till he nails it down. And believe you me, when he puts the hammer to it, it usually comes out in the right shape. Don't worry, Mr. Biddle. If it can be figured, Doc there'll cipher it right out. More hooch?"

Biddle refused a refill. "I have to meet my sister in a while. If she smells liquor on my breath . . ." He looked at Raider, who had turned a sad pale color. "Something wrong?"

No, Raider thought, I just humped Abby til her eyes bugged out. In fact, I was pluggin' her when ol' Morton got it in the next room.

Raider felt his stomach turning. "No, I'm okay. Just a little hungry. Where can a man git a good breakfast around these parts?"

"That reminds me," Biddle said, ignoring the big man's question. "I want to invite you and your partner to dinner tonight. Abby insists that she wants to prepare a home-cooked meal for both of you. Of course, my daughter won't be present. After that . . . well, that awful business, I sent her back east to live with one of her aunts."

Raider felt feverish. "Aw, I ain't sure we can—"

"Nonsense," Biddle replied. "We'll expect you around seven. Your partner should have some answers by then. Of course, if he comes up with anything before then, have him contact me immediately. Are you sure you're all right, Raider?"

The big man belched. "Yeah, I'm fine. Just this whiskey. I ain't exactly used to the good stuff."

Biddle clapped him on the shoulder. "A home-cooked meal will set you straight. Good day, sir."

Raider tipped his hat as Biddle left the table. The big Pinkerton from Arkansas wasn't thinking about food at all. Instead, his mind held the vivid image of Abigail Biddle's fleshy breasts. And a small voice beside that image kept whispering that her inviting tits were nothing but trouble.

Raider tapped lightly at Doc's door and listened for a reply. When the man from Boston didn't answer, Raider knocked harder. It was almost seven o'clock, the appointed hour for dinner at the Biddle household. The big man didn't relish the idea of facing Abigail without his partner to chaperon. Another tryst with the busty widow might complicate things greatly.

"Doc? You in there?"

"Go away," came the reply.

"Doc, it's time to go over to—"

The door swung open, startling Raider. Doc stood in the threshold with a peculiar look on his face, like he was scared or something. "Didn't you hear me? I said to go away."

"What about dinner? Look at me, I put on my suit again."

Doc waved him off. "Raider, I'll be there shortly. I just have to go over a few more details."

Raider tried to peer over his partner's shoulder. "What you working on in there?"

"Please, don't ask me. Just go to Biddle's house and stall him for a few hours. I'll be along shortly."

Doc slammed the door. Raider twirled his Stetson in his hands, wondering what had made his partner so spooky. He shrugged and started down the stairs, contemplating what lay ahead for him at the widow's dinner table.

Freemont Biddle met him at the door. Surprised to find

Raider alone, he inquired as to Doc's whereabouts. Raider assured his host that Doc would be along as soon as he was finished. Then the big man tried to get out of dinner, but Biddle wouldn't hear of it.

"Abigail has gone to a lot of trouble," the old gentleman replied. "She would be very disappointed if someone didn't eat her dinner."

Raider pulled at his collar, prompting Biddle to remark that he was certainly sweating a great deal for such a cool night.

Raider tried to smile when he said, "I just ain't used to wearin' a monkey suit twice in one week."

Biddle did not seem to hear him. He ushered Raider into a fine dining room where the table had been set for four. As a man used to the trail, Raider wondered how people could live in such a fancy setting. Civilized finery seemed like it would choke a man if he was cramped in by it. A wide-open plain was all a man really needed.

"So good of you to come . . . Mr. Raider, isn't it?"

Abigail Biddle had entered the room carrying a tray of fried chicken. Raider breathed easier when he saw that her bosom was covered. A wink from one of her green eyes went undetected by her brother.

"I hope you have an appetite," she said. "Free, will you please sit down and open the wine?"

Freemont Biddle started out of the room. "I'm not hungry right now."

"Er, don't leave us," Raider said too quickly.

Biddle turned halfway around. "I'm only interested in what your partner has to say. When he arrives, call me."

He was gone before Raider could offer further protestations.

Abigail Biddle set the platter of chicken on the table. "It appears that you and I are going to be alone for dinner. I must admit, Raider, I prefer it that way. Sit down. Don't be afraid of me."

Raider obeyed her, flopping down into a cushioned chair. He kept his eyes off the widow, focusing on the tableful of food. Abby had gone all out to prepare a typically Southern dinner—chicken, mashed potatoes, gravy, biscuits, greens, black-eyed peas, and cornbread. Raider decided he was hungry after all.

"Don't be shy," urged his hostess. "I know you're a lusty sort."

Raider replied by biting into a crisp chicken leg. He figured if he spent the evening in front of his plate, Doc would arrive before the widow could employ the schemes behind those devious green eyes. Not that a little tumble wouldn't have been a fitting end to the evening—it was just the wrong time, the wrong place, and the wrong woman.

But he couldn't eat enough. By the time his belly was full, Doc still hadn't knocked on the front door. And Abby was casting not-so-furtive glances in his direction. She wanted to be dessert.

Leaning toward him, she spoke in a breathy whisper. "I can't stop thinking about our . . . about the closet. I know that's wicked, since Hollis Morton was killed and all. But I haven't been able to take my mind off that glorious prize between your legs."

"Shh," Raider said. "You want your brother to hear? We got enough trouble without gettin' him mad at me."

Abby just smiled and started to loosen the buttons of her dress.

"Are you loco?" Raider said. "Not here!"

Her hand closed around his. "Then let's go somewhere else."

He drew back. "We can't do it, not now, not ever again. I wasn't thinkin' that night. Hell, we was lucky to get out of there without ever'body knowin' what we done. I had to make a damned stupid story, and Doc knew I was lyin'."

She sank down, disappearing beneath the table.

"Hey, what the hell are you . . . Abby!"

She crawled to him, digging at his crotch with playful hands. Raider stood up, aware that he was becoming excited. Abby's fingers stroked the rigid length inside his fancy suit pants.

The big man knew he had to flee. "I better get the hell out of here."

"Stop!" she cried. "If you leave, I'll tell my brother about what we were doing while Hollis Morton was being killed."

He turned back toward her, his eyes narrowed. "Listen, woman, don't be steppin' heavy on a fresh grave. Let the dead be. Don't bring 'em back with your nasty mouth."

She climbed out from under the table, pouting like a schoolgirl. "I never get to have any fun." She was on the verge of tears.

Raider took a step in her direction. "Aw, now, don't start jackin' the pump handle and get the water started."

She grabbed his crotch again. "The only handle I want to pump is between your legs. Let's go into the pantry."

Raider probably would have followed her if the knock had not resounded from the front door. Abby wanted him to ignore it, but he knew it was probably Doc. Sure enough, Biddle came down to answer the door, ushering in the man from Harvard. Abby fled quickly to the pantry, leaving Raider to get his urges under control. He hoped no one noticed his flustered condition.

When Doc came in with Biddle, the big man knew instantly that there was trouble. He saw it in his partner's eyes. What the hell had he found in that strongbox?

"Do you have any brandy?" Doc asked.

Biddle brought a flagon, and Doc had several quick snorts. Raider had never seen him put it away so fast. When he had finished drinking, Doc turned to his host.

"Mr. Biddle, I want you to summon the marshal and Hardy Tabor, if he is still in town. I think they should be here for this."

Raider started for the hat rack. "I'll go. Where's the marshal live? And where's Tabor stayin'?"

Biddle urged Raider away from the hat rack. "I'll send my stable boy. He can find the marshal, and the marshal can find Tabor."

When Biddle had left the room, Raider looked at his partner. "Doc, what you got to say about all this?"

Doc turned as pale as the froth on a white-water river. "I think I should wait until we are all assembled, Raider. What I have to tell you is something that I only want to repeat one time."

"Can't you at least tell me?"

"Once," Doc said curtly. "And then . . . if I'm lucky, perhaps you won't think I am totally insane."

"Sure, Doc, whatever you say. Have another brandy."

Raider watched his partner as he gulped down a healthy shot of liquor. Why the hell were Doc's fingers trembling? The big man decided to have a shot of brandy himself.

CHAPTER SIX

All eyes were on Doc Weatherbee. The man from Boston paced back and forth in front of Raider, Freemont Biddle, and Hardy Tabor. The marshal hadn't come to the meeting in Biddle's private study. It was Friday night in San Antonio, a time when any other cowboy was busy wetting his whistle and looking for some female company. A lot of those cowboys would be locked up before the night was over.

Doc reached into his coat pocket, removing a sheaf of papers that he held up for inspection by his anxious audience. "Remember one thing, gentlemen, what I am about to tell you is strictly conjecture on my part, theories I have calculated using the contents of Hollis Morton's strongbox."

Freemont Biddle wiped his beaded forehead with a handkerchief. "Confound it, Weatherbee, you're acting as if you're about to deliver the Holy Word."

Doc tossed the packet of papers onto Biddle's desk. "There, have a look for yourself, sir. And when you're through, come to my hotel and we will compare notes."

"No need for that tone, Weatherbee!" Biddle was red-faced.

Doc had his hands on his hips. "You wanted me to take charge of this matter, Mr. Biddle, and I have done so. Now you can either hear me out or you can dismiss me. You have my word when I say that this is not a task that I cherish.

Indeed, I would rather not say what I must."

Biddle leaned back, defeatedly wide-eyed. Raider was squinting at his partner. Doc seemed as jumpy as a thieving possum on a hot stove.

The big man glared at Biddle. "I think we better listen up on what my partner has to say, Freemont."

Tabor rejoined, "I wholeheartedly agree."

Biddle threw up his hands and sighed. "You have the floor, Weatherbee."

Doc lifted the bundle of papers from the desk top. "Hollis Morton, God rest his soul, had some interesting correspondence hidden in his strongbox. He received a great many letters from a man whose signature consisted of three initials: E.M.F. Mr. Biddle, did Morton ever mention a nephew who might possibly have a name coinciding with those three initials?"

Biddle shook his head. "Why, could this man be the murderer?"

"Perhaps," Doc replied. "Although the death of Hollis Morton, tragic though it may be, is no longer the single consideration here."

Tabor's brow wrinkled. "What could be more heinous than taking a man's life?"

"The death of a legend, Mr. Tabor." Doc unfolded a brown, tattered piece of parchment. "Before I can go on, I have to read this document, which may or may not be authentic."

Raider eyed the leathery paper. "Is it from that E.M. person?"

"No," Doc replied. "It's dated February twentieth, eighteen thirty-six."

Tabor looked up. "That's three days before Santa Anna began his siege of the Alamo."

"This communiqué concerns that very battle. If you'll allow me to read it to you." Doc stepped closer to the gas lamp, holding the parchment in the light. "It was intended for someone named Frazier. The first name has worn away with time. A simple message: 'Ambushed Mexican coach. Heading north toward the Alamo. Must get gold to Colonel Houston.' It was signed by a man named Morton."

Biddle slammed his fist on his desk. "What is that supposed to mean? Traipsing through the past when a good man lies dead and cold!"

Doc refolded the letter carefully and looked at Biddle. "If this message is genuine, then we can assume that it means a group of freedom fighters, commanded by this Morton, procured a Mexican gold shipment. They wanted to get it back to the Alamo and then on to Sam Houston. It would have no doubt aided his final stand against the Mexican army."

Tabor's eyes were frozen on the letter. "Is it true?"

Doc shrugged. "I was going to ask you if there was some way that we could obtain documentation that might—"

Biddle waved his handkerchief. "Histories of the Mexican War are inaccurate for the most part. Records are sparse. Besides, Weatherbee, I don't see what all of this has to do with the death of my good friend. I'm hiring you to solve that mystery, not a fifty-year-old pile of gibberish."

Tabor was looking at Biddle. "Freemont, you fought in the war against Santa Anna. Did you ever hear such a tale of gold being captured right before the Alamo battle?"

Biddle's patience seemed to be fraying. "I remember nothing except that my friend's funeral is tomorrow morning."

Doc leveled his eyes at the petulant old gentleman. "Sir, shall I continue, or would you like to go over the material and draw your own conclusions?"

Biddle grunted and leaned back in his chair.

Doc picked up four letters that were written on the same kind of stationery. "These were all mailed within the last year. All addressed to Hollis Morton and signed E.M.F. In the first letter, E.M.F. mentions that they had met, that they had discussed a matter of urgency. He ends the communiqué with these words: 'You should consider it. You know that it should belong to us now.' And he closes by saying that he will be in contact with Morton again."

"What is supposed to belong to this man and to Morton?" Biddle asked.

"I'll get to that," Doc replied. "As Aristotle said, every drama must have a beginning, a middle, and an ending."

Tabor agreed diplomatically. "We can't buck Aristotle."

"The second letter," Doc said, holding it up. "E.M.F.

chides Morton for not replying. He says he will be in San Antonio soon, to speak to Morton again. He makes a request for more money, as if Morton had given him something on their first meeting."

Raider twirled his Stetson on his fingers. "Blackmail?"

"A safe assumption," Doc replied.

"But what did this E.M.F. have on Morton?"

Doc went as white as a Rocky Mountain avalanche. He held up the third letter. "This is the most difficult thing to believe. For herein lies the connection to the message from fifty years ago, forty-seven to be exact. In this third communiqué, E.M.F. claims that the gold never got to Sam Houston. According to this man, the gold was taken to the Alamo, but it was seized at gunpoint by two of the men who were among the hundred and eighty-odd Texas volunteers. The two men in turn absconded with the treasure before the Mexican army advanced on the mission."

Tabor raised an eyebrow. "I wonder if two men could have gotten through the Mexican lines?"

Doc thumped the letter with the back of his hand. "This claims that the two thieves left the Alamo and headed east, sneaking around the right flank of Santa Anna's troops. When they reached the coast, he claims, they went south, deep into Mexico where no one would ever find them."

"Preposterous!" Biddle cried. "How could this man E.M.F. know about such things?"

Doc shrugged. "Perhaps he heard the story from some other member of the family. Something like this bears repeating."

Raider chortled. "Well, he sure as hell didn't hear it from somebody who fought at the Alamo. It took Santa Anna almost two weeks, but he finally managed to kill 'em all."

Doc looked at the letter again. The man from Boston was stonefaced. "The fourth letter, gentlemen. I'd like to read one thing to you. In this passage, E.M.F. implicates two men as the culprits who fled from the Alamo with Mexican gold. 'Those scoundrels,' he says, 'robbed gold that was captured by my great-uncle, your own brother. The colonel with his famous knife and the Kentucky politician ran with blood money. A king's treasure that belongs to our family since it did not reach its rightful place.'"

Raider's black eyes were bulging. Biddle clinched his chest. Tabor's jaw hung open with disbelief.

"Yes, gentlemen," Doc said. "The colonel with his knife —Colonel Jim Bowie. The Kentucky politician—Davy Crockett. According to the man who wrote these letters, two of Texas's most beloved folk figures absconded to safety to live out their days as rich men."

Raider laughed derisively. "Shee-it."

Tabor peered at the letters as if he wanted to burn them. "Can this be true?"

Biddle coughed for a long time before pouring himself a brandy.

Raider glared at Doc. "All right, say this boy writin' the letters is right—which he ain't. But let's say he is. How does he know they went to Mexico? And why would he go on and kill Morton?"

Doc nodded, as if he approved of Raider's question. "Morton was killed because he would not finance an expedition to Mexico, to recover whatever might be left of the treasure. As for Mexico . . ." Doc took out the paper that Raider had found on the roof of the warehouse, where the murderer had escaped so easily. "The lines on this paper correspond with all known maps of Mexico. The 'T' could stand for Tampico. The ink blob here could stand for the position of the treasure, or at least where the men fled when they left the mission."

Raider shook his head, chuckling. "Ain't that a good one! Davy Crockett and Jim Bowie, traitors to the state of Texas. This boy must have been chewin' some locoweed or drinkin' bad whiskey. Ever'body knows the colonel and Davy went down fightin' like the rest of them volunteers."

Freemont Biddle rose out of his chair. "Gentlemen, I'll not sit here and have you besmirch two of the finest names in Texas history."

He waddled toward the door of the study. Tabor started to stop him, but Doc waved him off. When Biddle was gone, Doc closed the door again.

Tabor eyed Doc suspiciously. "What are you up to, Weatherbee?"

"Nothing," replied the man from Boston. "I thought we

could talk more freely if Mr. Biddle were not here."

Tabor threw out his hands. "You aren't seriously considering this batch of nonsense as if were the truth?"

Doc held up a finger. "One, either it is the truth—"

"Never!"

Two fingers. "Or someone has gone to great lengths to fabricate a hoax in order to bilk Mr. Hollis Morton out of expedition money."

Raider slipped his hat over his head. "I vote for that."

"I second it," Tabor said.

A curious expression came over Doc's face. "Let's say it is true . . . just for a moment. If the killer believes it, then he might be going south to Mexico to try to find this treasure."

Tabor's nostrils flared. "That story cannot be true. Why, even if they were still alive, Davy Crockett and Jim Bowie would be as old as Biddle there. Older!"

Raider had his black squint aimed at Doc. "But if this boy is onto the truth, that gold might still be down there." Then he laughed. "Gold, hell! That's about the stupidest story I ever heard. Men like Crockett and Bowie didn't give a damn about gold."

Doc reached into his pocket. "Then tell me if you believe in this, my friend." He tossed something to Raider.

The yellow shine of gold was unmistakable under the gaslight. Raider snatched the gold piece out of the air. "Mexican, all right," the big man said.

Tabor grabbed the coin from his hands. "Let me see that."

"The date," Doc said.

"Eighteen thirty-five," Tabor replied softly. "A year before the Alamo."

Doc sighed. "I didn't really want to show that to Mr. Biddle. He is a veteran of the Texas War for Independence, after all."

Raider suddenly looked as if someone had kicked him squarely in the ribs. "Hell, Doc, you mean to tell me you actually believe this bull?"

Doc took the coin from Tabor, examining it one last time. "A man is dead. We have these letters, some gold, and a bizarre narrative, to say the least. I can't vote yes or no to this until I've had a chance to look further into the particulars. As of now, I can see arguments for both cases."

"How?" Tabor asked.

Doc shrugged. "On one side, who can doubt the honesty of two men like Davy Crockett and Jim Bowie? On the other, there's no exact count on the number of volunteers who died at the Alamo. Who's to say that two men could not have gotten out of there with a chest full of gold? Can anyone really prove that two of our country's godlike heroes were among the dead when Santa Anna gave the orders to slaughter those brave souls?"

Tabor's eyelids flickered nervously as he spoke. "We don't want this to get around, gentlemen. I'd like to talk to the governor personally about this matter. Would it be possible to convince you to stay in San Antonio for a day or two, until I can get my thoughts clear?"

"You have but to wire our agency and request us to remain on this case," Doc replied.

Tabor stood up, extending his hand. "Consider yourself employed by the State of Texas."

Raider still had a sly grin on his face. "I'm tellin' y'all, this ain't gonna come to a damn thing. Somebody is lyin' through their teeth."

Doc turned to his partner. "An accurate assessment, most probably. But how many times have we kicked a rock, only to have a snake whip out from beneath it?"

Tabor was finally able to smile again. "Your partner has a point, Mr. Raider. But let's keep all of this under our hats until you hear from me again." He glanced at the letters on Biddle's desk. "What about those?"

Doc tossed the bundle to Tabor. "I have my notes. Burn them if you like. Show them to the governor. File them away. They can only hurt the dead, not the living."

"They sure as hell hurt Hollis Morton," Raider replied. "Right through the damned throat."

A knock at the door dispelled the eerie silence that had come over them. Abigail Biddle stuck her head through the doorway. "My brother has retired for the evening, fine sirs. But he has extended his hospitality if you gentlemen would like to stay and talk. May I get you something?" She was looking straight at Raider.

The big man wondered if Doc would notice the gleam in the widow's eye.

Tabor bowed to Abigail. "I'm afraid I must be going, Miss Biddle. If you gentlemen will excuse me? Until we meet again."

"Soon," Doc replied. "And make sure you wire the agency immediately, before they assign us to another case."

Tabor nodded, hurrying out of the study.

Abby smiled again. "Would you like some coffee, Raider?"

"How 'bout some whiskey?"

Doc shook his head. "No drinking on the job. We have things to discuss. Coffee will be fine, Miss Biddle."

Did Doc see the wink in her green eyes? Why she was doing everything in her power to show his partner that they had been lovebirds? Didn't she know there were enough complications already?

Doc seemed undaunted as he regarded Raider. "Your thoughts about this unlikely fantasy?"

Raider pulled his hat down low over his eyes. "Danged me if I know. Them letters is kinda . . . what's the word?"

"Obvious," Doc replied.

"That's it. And this E.M.F. must be a pretty excitable fella to stab his own kin. Fishy as hell."

The gentleman Pinkerton nodded. "But that gold piece is undeniable."

"It's Mex all right. Maybe even went through the hands of Santa Anna himself. Doc, what if it's true? What if Crockett and Bowie decided they wanted to take a sack full of gold and git out? I know I feel like that sometimes. Remember when all that gold and money was flyin' out over the plain, in that wind? I thought to myself then, I could just pick it up and sock it away. Work for another year and go back to where I hid it."

"But you didn't," Doc said.

"No, I sure didn't."

"And you aren't nearly cut out of the same fabric as a Jim Bowie or a Davy Crockett."

Raider scowled at his dandified partner. "The hell you say. Why, if I'da been at the Alamo, I'da gone down shootin' like the rest of them. You woulda done it too, Doc. A certain kinda man ain't afraid of dyin' if he knows he's right and fightin' for a good cause."

"Precisely," Doc replied. After a moment, he said, "I'll make inquiries tomorrow. Perhaps I can uncover something about Hollis Morton's other blood relatives."

At that moment, Abigail Biddle chose to make her entrance with a tray of hot coffee. "Here we are, Raider."

Doc gathered up the remainder of his notes. "I should be running along. I'll leave my partner to have coffee with you."

"Maybe I should go too, Doc!" The big man started to rise, but Abby pushed him down.

"Enjoy your coffee," Doc called as he headed for the front door.

Abby thrust a cup into Raider's hand. "Would you like me to sweeten it with brandy?"

"Hell, why not?"

He looked into her green eyes, wondering why Doc had practically given him permission to stay with Abby. Maybe his partner had too much on his mind to be worried about small details. Raider figured he could use a diversion. Watching the rise and fall of Abby's chest, he was almost sure he had found one.

Freemont Biddle had been wrong in his assessment of the historical accounts of the Texas War for Independence from Mexico. Doc stayed up long into the night, reading by gaslight, fascinated by the legend of the Alamo. The word *alamo* was the Spanish name for the cottonwood tree. Just a small mission in a cottonwood stand. A symbol of freedom for every citizen north of the Rio Grande.

In December of 1835, a band of approximately one hundred and eighty men, led by Colonel James Bowie, attacked Mexican forces at San Antonio occupying the Alamo. The Texas volunteers held the mission until February of 1836, when four thousand of Santa Anna's men moved up from the south. The volunteers held off the Mexican army for twelve days, dealing Santa Anna more than a thousand casualties. When the Alamo was finally overrun by Mexican troops, no prisoners were taken. A slaughter.

Doc looked up from the book, resting his eyes. He wondered if two men carrying a chest of gold could have slipped through Santa Anna's line of soldiers. The imagined feat had a certain bravado about it—as if two men like Bowie and Crockett could have pulled it off. But no! They were great men. Their stand at the Alamo weakened Santa Anna's advance and allowed Sam Houston to mount his defense. The men of the Alamo had not died in vain. Doc closed the book.

He reached for the stub of a cigar and fired the red-coal tip. He reached up to turn out the gaslight. Sometimes he could think better in the dark. He let his imagination run wild with all sorts of premises, none of which jelled into anything plausible. So he had to forget about the wild story of the Alamo and go back to the fact that he had a murder on his hands. A murder committed by a man who might still be in San Antonio.

Doc's mind worked until he fell asleep in his chair. Then he was lost in a confusing dreamworld, chasing a man in a black hood. He woke up quickly when the hooded dream man turned back and started to chase him.

"Wait a minute. Now, tell me how this feels."

Raider looked up at the dark ceiling. Abby was doing things to him. She seemed to be having a good old time of it. She wouldn't let him fall asleep.

Abby glanced up at him, but she couldn't see his face. "Well?"

"Well what?"

Her hands were where her mouth had been. "How did that feel just now? Did you like it?"

Raider sighed. "Yeah, I reckon it was all right." He yawned, hoping she would give up. But she was like a snapping turtle—once she got hold of something, she wouldn't let go until it thundered.

Her head was between his legs. "Here, how about this?"

She did something that caused a chill to run through Raider's body, stoking a fire in every cell of his six-foot, three-inch frame. He let her do it until he couldn't stand it anymore. She laughed when he pushed her head away.

Her hand massaged his revived member. "Looks like that thing is alive again. Want to do it?"

Suddenly he wanted to do it real bad. He started to roll over. She resisted, still full of surprises.

"Let me try it on top."

Raider surrendered without a fight.

Abby straddled him, guiding him inside, laughing as she rode his cock like a pony. He watched her breasts as they shook above him. He exploded almost immediately. Abby fell on top of him, smothering his face with her bosom. Raider rolled her off and grabbed the pillow.

"Hey," she said, "I wasn't finished."

"Well, you done finished me, honey." Raider buried his face in the satin pillowcase. "Let me get some shut-eye, and we'll mix it up in the mornin'."

"Oh, all right."

She snuggled into his back, pushing those taut nipples into his skin. Raider started to drift off. Then he felt her hand, groping mischievously for his cock.

"Abby..."

Someone screamed. Her hand was gone. She looked up over Raider's shoulder.

"It's my brother."

Raider grabbed his coat on the end of the bedpost. His hand came up with the derringer. He stepped into his pants and started for the bedroom door. Freemont Biddle cried out again.

Abby slipped up beside the big man. "He hollers in his sleep sometimes. It's nothing to worry about."

"I better take a look."

Raider sidled into the hall, creeping toward the bedroom at the other end of the corridor. He could hear Biddle tossing in a fitful dream. As he neared the old man's bedchamber, the words became intelligible.

"Damn you... damn you to hell... Morton... no, Morton, no."

Probably dreaming about his old friend. Raider turned back toward Abby's room. Again the sleeping man uttered a strange phrase, causing the big Pinkerton to hesitate.

"Frazier!" Biddle moaned. "The gold, Frazier, the gold. Ours... ours. No, Frazier, no..."

He had heard all of that from Doc. Or had he? Maybe

Biddle knew more than he was telling. Hadn't the state man said that Biddle fought in the Texas War for Independence?

"Raider, come on back to bed."

Abby stood in the hallway with a flannel gown draped around her.

Raider hurried back to her room. But instead of undressing, he found the rest of his clothes. Abby was obviously hurt that he was leaving.

"Can't you stay a little longer?"

Raider shook his head, pulling on his right boot. "I don't want to be around here when your brother wakes up. He might not take to me spendin' the night."

Abby struck a match and torched the end of a candle. Raider could see that she was pouting. He reached up and took her hand.

"We had some night, didn't we, Abby?"

She shook her head, still solemn.

"Hey, now don't be like that. You and me, we come from different sides of the river."

"Oh, just go soak your head in that river!" Abby cried.

She threw a pillow at him and ran away into another chamber of the dark house. Raider pulled on his shirt and then grabbed his coat. He tiptoed down the hall, pausing for a moment at Biddle's door. The old man was snoring.

Raider was halfway down the stairs when he heard Biddle mutter the name "Morton" again. What the hell did that mean? Raider wondered if he should tell Doc. Maybe the man from Boston could put all of the jagged pieces together. Somebody had to try.

As he reached for the knob of the front door, a hand closed around his arm. He caught the scent of Abby's perfume, the only thing that kept him from swinging a blow into the darkness. She pressed her body against him.

"How'd you get down here so fast?" he asked.

She giggled. "Back stairs. I didn't want you to leave if you were angry with me."

"Aw, I ain't mad," Raider replied.

She kissed him for a long time before she would let go. Raider gave her final pat on the rump. She grabbed the door when it was half open.

"Will I see you again, Raider?"

He tried to sound official. "I don't know, Abby. I'm gonna be helpin' Doc on this murder thing."

"Oh, yes. That was so horrible, wasn't it?"

"Goodbye, Abby."

"No, just farewell. If you don't find me, Raider, I'll find you."

Raider escaped into the night, closing the door behind him.

The air was still. It had to be near dawn. A chill caught him in the shoulders, running out into his arms and down his spine. He checked the derringer in his pocket.

Something squawked behind him. He looked up at the second story of the house. Had it been some night bird of prey? Or had Freemont Biddle cried out again in his sweaty nightmares?

Raider spun and started for the hotel, using his long strides to outdistance the lingering shadows of the night.

CHAPTER SEVEN

A palm of hot night air moved up from the south, making for a dry, sweaty evening in San Antonio. Doc and Raider stood with their backs to the breeze, peering at the chapel of the Mission San Antonio de Valero—the Alamo to anyone with even a sketchy knowledge of history, Texan and American. Allan Pinkerton's most daring pair of detectives had been combing the grounds all day, sifting through the structures that had survived since the early years of the eighteenth century. They found little more than the obvious signs of the last occupants, the U.S. Army, which had quartered troops and stored supplies in the sun-dried brick buildings some thirty-odd years before.

Raider pushed his hat onto the back of his head. "Can't have a square dance without a fiddler, Doc."

"Quiet, I'm thinking."

But what was there to think about? They had not heard from Tabor, who had been gone for three days. Nor had the search for Hollis Morton's relatives been productive. As far as Doc knew, with Texas state records included, Hollis Morton had been a loner. He had even married a woman who was without family, a schoolteacher named Emily Johnston. The kinship alleged by the letter-writing man could not be proven, at least in the Lone Star state.

Raider shifted impatiently, toeing the ground with his boot.

"I mean, hell, Doc, except for that wire from the home office tellin' us to stay put, we ain't struck a lick at a snake."

Doc shook his head. "If we haven't heard from Tabor by Friday, I'll request that Wagner take us off this case."

"What case?"

For once Doc shared Raider's indifference. Not that he was shirking the job of solving the mystery. It was the solution that scared him, the thought that he might be responsible for rewriting the history books and dropping mud on two legends of the West. In his entire career as a detective, he had rarely dreaded the resolution of a quandary so much.

Doc raised his hands, gesturing as if he were arranging the players on a dimly lighted stage. "I've been trying to imagine two men slipping away from Santa Anna's army. Would the others have let them go? Or did they lie and say they were going to try to get the gold to Sam Houston?"

Raider chortled skeptically. "I want to talk to the boy who signs them letters with three initials. I want him to tell me how he knows about all this stuff."

Doc took off his derby to fan himself. "How can we even suspect that the killer and the letter writer are the same man? It's a logical assumption, but not an ironclad fact."

"I don't know, Weatherbee. This whole thing sounds kinda stupid to me."

Doc sighed. "At any rate, we are bound by contract to search for the killer of Hollis Morton. Since this Alamo lead hasn't taken us any closer to the murderer's identity, I suggest we follow up what clues we have. One, the killer was extremely agile. Two, his middle name could be Morton. Three, he found out about the story of the Alamo gold."

Raider's black eyes gleamed for a moment. "Hey, we shoulda thunk of it before. There's probably a few old-timers around who coulda heard about that same . . ." The big man turned abruptly to his right, peering over his shoulder down the dim, dirt road.

Doc looked as well in the same direction, but he didn't see a thing. "What is it, Raider?"

"Harness. Four horses. Big wagon, coach or a—"

"I see it now."

Raider's hand slid easily to the butt of his Colt. "You

reckon it might be somebody looking for us?"

"Take care with that side arm. Don't go blowing holes in anyone unless it's absolutely necessary."

They watched quietly as the vehicle slowed near the main chapel of the mission. Doc recognized the coach as a George IV phaeton, no doubt purchased from the renowned Brewster and Company, Broome Street, New York. Bright twin lamps illuminated the driver's way as he pulled the coach to a halt in front of the Alamo.

A door on the carriage swung open. When a man stepped out into the light of the coachlamp, Raider's voice boomed through the night. "This is all closed up, mister. Turn that buggy around and get on out of here."

The reply came back: "I have the governor's permission."

"Tabor," Doc said. "And about damned time."

They joined him in the phaeton, which belonged to Freemont Biddle. The old man had let Tabor borrow it. "Freemont told me that you two were down here nosing around. Did you come up with anything?"

Doc shook his head. "Nothing. Just what you already know. And you?"

"Morton did have relations in Nebraska," Tabor replied. "But none of them followed him when he moved to Texas."

Raider, who couldn't extend his legs in the coach, frowned at the governor's assistant. "So you want us to head north and root around?"

Tabor hesitated, his hands suspended in midair. He dropped them and rubbed his thighs. Doc and Raider both saw it coming. He had to tell them something that would not be pleasant. They were about to get a job that nobody else wanted to do.

"Er, gentlemen . . ."

Raider scowled at the politician. "Doc's a gentleman, I'm just a cowboy. If you got something to say, Tabor, then cut loose."

Tabor leaned back against the plush leather upholstery of Biddle's fine carriage. "I've been with the governor for two days, my friends. He's concerned about these allegations, as is the senior senator of this great state. Now, both of you come highly recommended. I spoke to a lawyer up in Austin, a man named Greenly. He says you helped him when he was—"

"No soap necessary," Doc interrupted. "I must defer to my partner at this point. If you will simply tell us what you require."

Tabor exhaled the sentence like it was his last breath. "We want you to go to Mexico and see if there's any credence to this story."

Raider laughed. "Hell!"

Doc's blue eyes popped open. "An interesting proposition."

The big man glared at his partner. "Are you loco, Doc? Wagner'll never let us traipse off to Mexico."

Tabor reached inside his coat pocket. "Oh, but he will, Mr. Raider. I have a directive right here, ordering you to pursue the case of the Alamo treasure. Naturally we want you to discern the truth and bring it back to us. We'll decide what to do from there."

Doc looked irritated. "Mexico? But we haven't any jurisdiction down there."

"We've arranged a liaison officer," Tabor replied. "His name is Sanchez, Julio Sanchez. He's an officer in the army of General Porfirio Díaz, the . . . the head of the Mexican government."

"Dictator," Doc replied. "Isn't that a more accurate word?"

Tabor shrugged. "Díaz has helped his country. The railroads are running somewhat, and the mines are in operation."

Raider didn't like the sound of it. "So we're supposed to be runnin' around down there with just this Mexican soldier to say we got permission to find Davy Crockett and Jim Bowie?"

Tabor raised a finger. "Shh." He looked upward. "Driver, take us to Mr. Biddle's house immediately."

The driver called back, "What about them other horses?"

Tabor ordered him to tie their mounts to the back of the carriage. When that was done, they rolled through the uneven streets of San Antonio. For a while they were all silent.

Finally, Raider decided he had had enough. "I ain't goin'," he offered.

Doc shrugged. "I'm having my doubts as well."

Tabor flashed a diplomatic expression of concern. "If you

don't go, someone else will. Your superiors think if anyone can solve this, it's both of you. Of course, I needn't remind you of the higher stakes in this game. The names of two legends."

Raider kicked the seat opposite him. "Ever'time there's a stump to be dug up out of the cornfield, me and Doc are the first ones to get handed a shovel." He eyed the politician. "Why don't you come with us, Tabor? You might learn somethin'."

Tabor turned beet red. "I am not a detective, sir. I am serving my state the best way I know how. If you are accusing me—"

"He's accusing you of nothing," Doc said. "Mr. Tabor, if we decide to go, what shall we do if we find the gold in question? Providing that the story has some credence, of course."

"The treasure goes back to the Mexican government," Tabor replied. "That was the only way we could get them to agree to let both of you cross over the Mexican border."

Doc smiled. "So we're supposed to bring back the dignity of two American heroes."

Tabor nodded. "There isn't enough gold in the state of Texas to make up for the loss of those near-mythical figures. If you gentlemen decide to stay on the case, you'll be protecting the reputations of Davy Crockett and Jim Bowie. Wouldn't that be enough for you?"

Raider grunted. "You *had* to go an' say it, didn't you?"

Doc raised his finger. "Let us not forget Hollis Morton, who was slain for a lesser cause."

"No," Tabor said penitently, "we cannot forget Hollis Morton."

The carriage slid to a halt. "Mr. Biddle's, sir," the driver called.

Tabor challenged both Pinkerton operatives. "I appeal to your sense of patriotism, gentlemen. Can I count on you to accept this case?"

Doc requested a moment alone. When Tabor slipped through the door, the man from Boston looked at Raider. "Well?"

Raider took off his Stetson and ran a hand over his dark

hair. "You got me, Doc. If we don't go, it could mean a lot of train duty, or stagecoach ridin'. Wagner ain't gonna be happy."

Doc shrugged. "Since this is a government matter, they could send Texas Rangers or special agents from the governor's office. They could even bring in men from Washington."

Raider scoffed at the invocation of other agencies. "And what do you think them boys is gonna turn up?"

"Perhaps nothing, perhaps the same things we will find."

Raider smiled defeatedly. "Hell, I ain't been to Mexico for a long time. Gonna be hot down there."

Doc reached for the handle of the carriage door. "Then I can tell Tabor that we're going?"

"You want to, Doc?"

"I'm afraid I do. My curiosity has gotten the better of me. If you want to stay behind, I can request another partner."

Raider shook his head. "Count me in. I reckon I'm kinda like the cat myself. Course, you remember what curiosity did to him."

"I'll be a while," Doc said, ignoring his partner's pessimism. "I want to go over that map again. I also want to ask Freemont Biddle a few questions."

The big man frowned. "Don't tell him I said anything about him cryin' out in his sleep."

"Give me some credit for having a brain," Doc replied. "I'll see you back at the hotel. I'm sure the driver will take you directly there."

With that, Doc was gone, joining Tabor and Biddle in the big house.

Raider tapped on the wall of the coach. "Run me on back to the livery and then to the hotel."

"Yessir!"

The carriage rolled forward for a few yards and then stopped again.

Raider called to the driver, "Somethin' wrong?"

"Nosir!"

"Then why you stoppin' in the alley? Don't you know your way?"

The carriage door swung open. "Hello, Raider. I told you I'd find you before you left."

Abigail Biddle climbed into the seat opposite the big man.

Raider peered out of the shades that were drawn over the windows. He was scared somebody might see them together. "Abby, are you plumb crazy?"

She opened her cape, revealing the delicate alabaster globes of her bosom. "What a stroke of luck, your partner going inside with Tabor and my brother. When I saw him leave, I just threw on my cape and stopped the carriage. Oh, don't worry about the driver, he won't say anything. I'll give him a dollar to keep quiet."

"Abby, we can't—"

She slid into the seat beside him. Her hand went inside his denim shirt, feeling the thick hair on his chest. Raider looked straight down into the cleft of her bosom. He sure as hell didn't feel like telling her to get out of the coach.

"We can't go to my hotel, Abby. What'll ever'body say when they see us goin' upstairs?"

Abby kissed his ear. "Don't worry, we aren't going to the hotel."

Raider drew back a little. "We sure as hell can't go back to your house, not with Doc there." Not to mention her quarrelsome brother.

She freed her shoulders and her breasts from the top half of her dress. She guided Raider's fingers to her nipples. "Don't worry, cowboy, we're going to stay right here. Driver," she called out, "once around town. Stop for nothing."

Raider was aghast. "In the coach?"

The phaeton lurched forward.

Her palm rubbed the erection at his crotch. "In the coach. All you have to do is lift my dress."

As the rolled through the streets of San Antonio, Raider did just that.

As usual, Doc took care of the preliminaries, arranging their itinerary with some help from Tabor. They would take the railroad as far as Brownsville, and from there they would travel by water, sailing the Gulf of Mexico to Tampico and possibly beyond. Since the lengthy journey forced considerations of time and logistics, Doc was leaving his mule and wagon behind in San Antonio. Instead, he carried several boxes and bundles that bore all of the maps, tools, and specialties of a man with a great deal of scientific knowledge. Raider brought his bedroll, the clothes on his back, and his guns. He didn't care a damn for science, except when Doc used it to save their lives.

When they boarded the train the next afternoon, Tabor gave them a packet containing official letters of introduction and several thousand pesos in Mexican gold. "I'll await your findings," he shouted over the screeching whistle of the train.

Raider waved back as if he had heard. "I ain't been to Brownsville in a dog's age," the big man said to Doc, who sat opposite him in the compartment furnished by the State of Texas. "Leastways we're travelin' like rich men."

Doc ignored his partner, rustling a map in front of his face. "We aren't going to Brownsville, not directly. We're disembarking at San Benito and transporting our cargo to a place called Port Isabel."

"That's *your* cargo," Raider replied.

Doc put down the map. "Don't worry, Tabor has arranged for some horses and two men to help us to the ship."

Raider squinted at his partner. "What kinda ship is it?"

Doc shrugged. "I have no idea. Tabor took care of that."

"I just hope we don't have no trouble. Hell, we ain't even near Mexico yet." The big man pulled down the brim of his Stetson, covering his eyes. "I reckon I better try to get me some shut-eye."

Doc picked up the map again. "Yes, I'd rather hear you snoring than talking. You make more sense when you're asleep."

"Aw, to hell with you, Weatherbee."

Raider closed his eyes, thinking about one Miss Abigail Biddle, a widow who sort of grew on a man after a while. His musing turned into a dream. They were in the coach again and then back at the opera house. Then it all went black for a while, before Raider saw the man hovering over the body of Hollis Morton. He thought the man had grabbed him, but when he sat up in a cold sweat, he realized Doc was shaking him.

"We're here."

Raider gazed out of the dusty window into a patch of dark

that closed around a circle of lantern light. "We just left San Antone."

"Nine hours ago," Doc replied. "The train made good time through the night. You were sleeping the whole way."

Raider just shook his head. "Don't seem right to go to sleep in one place and wake up in another."

They stepped out of the train, toward a deserted-looking station.

Raider's hand tickled the butt of his Peacemaker. The air had a crispness to it, the dewy anticipation of dawn. The big man turned his head, looking for signs of movement.

"I ain't likin' this too much, Doc."

The man from Boston had his hand inside his coat pocket, gripping the handle of his .38 Diamondback. "Patience. We're early."

Something rattled to their left, behind a dilapidated platform.

Raider came up with the Colt. "Show yourself in the light."

A voice replied from the shadows, "Tabor sent y'all?"

"He did," Doc called.

Two men stepped forward, coming into the glow of the lantern that hung on the side of the boxcar. One of them led a team of packhorses. He stopped when he saw Raider's Colt.

"Ain't no need for that," the man said.

Raider holstered the pistol. "No, and there better not be any need for it."

Doc gestured toward the back half of the private car. "If you gentlemen will assist me."

Raider stood guard while they loaded up the packhorses. Not that there was any danger. The big man just found guarding easier than loading. He figured he wasn't getting paid to tote Doc's bundles.

When they were set, the train whistle sounded and the engine chugged on to Brownsville. Raider raised his collar against the chill of the air. "How come this station looks so ratty?"

"Train don't usually stop here," replied the man who had led the team of horses.

Raider noticed there were no mounts for riding. "You boys didn't bring no horses for us?"

The man jerked his head toward the east. "We can walk it. Be there before midday. It won't kill you."

Doc was afraid his partner might bristle at such impertinence, but the big man from Arkansas only nodded, like he knew walking really wouldn't kill him. They started out through a grove of evergreens, traversing a narrow, sandy path that led them toward the Gulf. As the sun rose in front of them, Doc began to smell the salt air. And just as the man had promised, by noontime they were gazing down at the steely waters of the Gulf of Mexico.

Raider put his hands triumphantly on his hips. "Hell, that wasn't too painful, now, was it?"

Doc frowned at the calm water. "My friend, we're just beginning."

Raider knew Doc was right, so he frowned too. Mexico was just a stone's throw away, but the answers they needed weren't really any closer. He looked back at the men who were unloading the packhorses.

"Y'all leavin'?"

"This was all we was paid to do, Pinkerton."

Doc nodded. "Thank you." He reached into a bundle and withdrew his telescope, extending it for a look out over the water. Nothing. He slapped the telescope together. "We'll have to wait for the boat."

Raider looked out over the sand dunes that stretched to the water's edge. "Kinda reminds me of Galveston. Don't it?"

Doc grimaced. "We had a great deal of trouble in Galveston."

"Yeah, but we took care of it."

"We did at that," Doc replied.

But they both still had that bad feeling in their guts. The feeling persisted until well into the afternoon. Then Doc spied the sail on the horizon. It was a small ship making for their quiet harbor.

"A sloop," Doc said.

"What?"

"Never mind."

The craft anchored about a half mile offshore. Doc

watched as the small dinghy was pulled up from its mooring behind the ship. A man got into the dinghy and rowed for shore. Doc figured the man at the oars was a mate on the sloop, but when the sea-crusty sailor pulled the dinghy onto the beach, he introduced himself as Lionel Crockett, skipper of the sloap *Creole Lady.*

"Crockett!" Raider cried. "Hey are you—"

"Later," Doc broke in. "Shall we load our baggage, Captain Crockett."

"Lionel," the sailor said.

He was smiling as he started for the pile of boxes.

Raider was grinning. "Crockett! You reckon . . . ?"

Doc shrugged. "We have but to ask."

Raider started after the captain, to help him with a cumbersome load. Suddenly the big man didn't have the bad feeling anymore. They were moving, on the case again. The way Doc started jumping around, Raider knew his partner had shaken the jitters as well. For the first time since the death of Hollis Morton, they were on top of things.

Standing at the tiller of his vessel, Captain Lionel Crockett cut a comical figure. His brown hair was red-streaked from the sun, as was his thick beard. He wore a bandanna tied over his pate, and wore faded blue trousers that had long ago surrendered to the bleaching effects of the sun. A bare, deep-tanned chest, clear eyes, a smile that comes from a clear-headed man who enjoys his life. Doc figured his age to be somewhere between thirty-five and forty years.

As the sloop drew away from Port Isabel, Texas, Doc and Raider moved to the aft section of the boat, near the tiller. They watched as Crockett directed his mate with hand signals. The smallish man scurried up to the mast with the agility of a monkey.

"He's quick, that one," Crockett said. "But deaf as a clam shell."

"Can't hear nothin'?" Raider asked.

The captain nodded. "Had to take him on in Galveston. My other man never came back from his liberty." Crockett laughed. "That one up there can't speak a word, but I'm learnin' how to talk without words."

With the breeze behind him, the sloop cut swiftly through the light chop on the Gulf. Both Pinkertons kept their eyes on the sailor. How were they going to ask him if he was related to Davy Crockett? If he had ever heard the bizarre story about the Alamo treasure?

Doc urged Raider on with a subtle tilt of the head. The big man smiled at the captain. "We just come down from San Antone. You ever been to San Antone, Lionel?"

"Can't say that I have," the sailor replied. "I stick close by the water. Get too far inland, things have a way of closin' up on you."

Doc jumped in. "We had the good fortune to visit the Alamo while we were . . . but say, isn't your surname Crockett? Why, you wouldn't be . . ."

The captain laughed. "Can't say as I am. Ever'body asks me if I was relations to that famous Crockett, Davy, you know. But the only Davy I know is a hundred fathoms down. Davy Jones's locker."

Raider frowned. "You mean you ain't never heard no family stories about a man who mighta been your own cousin?"

Crockett shrugged. "My people hail from Georgia. I grew up in Savannah myself."

Doc sighed. "A pity. A great deal of our investigation hinges on a certain unbelievable story about Davy Crockett. If we could only find out a few necessary facts . . ."

The captain's eyes reflected a reddish sky. "Well, now, I reckon I've heard nearly ever' tale there is about that man."

Raider leaned closer toward the captain. "What's that you say?"

"Since me and Davy Crockett got the same name, people just up and tell me different tales about him. You know, tall tales. Mostly lies, I'm thinkin'."

Doc exchanged glances with his partner. Raider nodded. Doc braced himself against the rail of the sloop. "Captain, would you like to listen to another story and then perhaps tell us if you've heard it before?"

Crockett replied, "I'm here to help y'all the best I can."

After a moment of hesitation, Doc told him the story about Davy Crockett and Jim Bowie allegedly leaving the Alamo with a king's ransom in gold.

The captain's face went slack. "Can't rightly say as I've heard that one." He glanced up to see his mate staring back at them. Crockett waved him toward the bow. "Sometimes I think he can hear ever' word I say."

"Want to test him?" Raider asked.

When the captain nodded, Raider pulled his Colt and fired a shot into the air. The mate didn't flinch.

"Guess he can't hear," Crockett said.

Doc looked irritated. "Captain, are you sure you haven't—"

"I ain't even heard the story you done told me," Crockett replied. "See, if I ain't heard it, I can't tell nobody else now, can I?"

"No," Doc replied. "I suppose you can't."

"I'm to get you to Tampico," he continued. "Then you can buy yourself some pack animals and take it from there by your lonesome."

Raider tipped back his Stetson. "Didn't mean to rile you, Lionel. I don't believe that story any more'n you do."

"Ain't heard no story," Crockett replied.

They were running parallel to a declining, coppery sun on the starboard side of the sloop. A cool Gulf breeze pushed them southward. Raider didn't know it, but they were crossing the Brazos Santiago Pass, where the Rio Grande emptied into the gulf. They were already in Mexican waters, but still a long way from Tampico and the old Indian man who would give them so many incredible answers.

CHAPTER EIGHT

"You sure that's Tampico, Captain?"

Raider dropped the telescope from his eye and looked at Lionel Crockett. The big man wanted it to be Tampico. He wanted to get off the boat. He was tired of the sea, the endless stretching of the water, the fish they ate every night when the deaf-mute pulled them in on a frayed handline. He hated the nausea in the pit of his gut, the seasickness that came with the rocking of the sloop.

The captain nodded. "Ain't rightly Tampico on the shore, but she's inland. You're lookin' at the mouth of the Panuco River. Tampico is upstream a mile or two."

Doc took the glass from his partner. He was growing tired of the voyage himself. The days seemed to blend together, one after another, forcing him to keep a written record so he could be sure of the date.

"How far upriver can we take the sloop?" asked the man from Boston.

Lionel Crockett rubbed his beard. "Can't say, except that I ain't goin' upriver with you."

Raider scowled at the brown-skinned sailor. "Hell, Captain, we been on this boat for more'n a week. Now you say you're gonna desert us right when we need you the most."

Crockett never wavered. "I was paid to take you as far as

Tampico. I'll swing in and you can take the dinghy. Don't even have to bring her back."

Raider shook his head in disgust. "Hell, if that ain't the most chicken-shit thing I ever—"

Doc waved him off. "Raider, the good captain has done his duty. We must proceed from here on our own."

"It ain't like I'm scared," Crockett said. "I'm swingin' down to Tuxpan, pickin' up a small load of salt mackerel, takin' it back up to Brownsville. I might be back this way in a month. Look for me from the beach."

"Assuredly," Doc said. "Assuredly."

The sloop caught the influx of the tide, swinging around into the natural mouth of the harbor. Doc's goods were loaded into the dinghy, which appeared close to sinking under the weight. With Doc and Raider added to the cargo, the small vessel was barely navigable.

Captain Crockett peered over the bow of the sloop. "You boys take her easy. I'll be lookin' for you when I swing—what the devil?"

The deaf-mute crewman had flown past his captain, diving overboard. He swam to the edge of the dinghy and looked up at Doc and Raider, making noises like he wanted to come along.

Doc glanced at his partner. "Seems we have a convert, Raider."

The big man looked down into the lad's anxious face. "I reckon he's as ready to be off that boat as I am."

Doc went through an elaborate series of signs that told the deaf man he wouldn't be paid very much if he came along. The lad nodded. "I don't think we have enough room in this boat. How will he—"

As if he had understood, the deaf-mute kicked around to the backside of the dinghy. He splashed his feet in the water, indicating that he would help power the boat from behind. Raider said if the kid wanted to come along that badly, he was welcome. They could use the extra hand.

"Welcome aboard," Doc said, tipping his derby.

Captain Lionel Crockett was laughing on the deck of the sloop. "So long, you lunatics. May the tide run your way."

Doc gripped the oars of the dinghy. "We're ready, I suppose."

Raider's eyes were fixed on the beaches to the right and left of the river's mouth. "Let's get the hell off the water, Doc."

Remembering his days on crew at Harvard, Doc began to pull at the oars, moving the dinghy toward the muddy port of Tampico.

"Jesus, Doc, looks like a damned hurricane has been through here."

Raider was peering toward the port proper of Tampico. The waterfront consisted of slipshod, slapdash wooden structures that appeared to be ready to surrender at any moment to the force of gravity. A writhing beehive mass of humanity moved between the structures, busily at work to sustain life for another day. The people were as brown and worn as the shacks on the riverbank. Many of them stopped to look at the boatload of white men who rowed toward a rickety dock.

Doc kept his eyes trained on the blank, dirty faces that scrutinized their movements. "I wasn't expecting a welcoming committee."

Raider touched his Colt, which was showing some rust from the salt air. "You know somethin'? I'd just as soon be somewhere else right now."

"Easy," Doc replied. "The last thing you want to do is show fear or hostility."

Doc guided the dinghy even with the dock. The high-water mark had been covered by the incoming tide, allowing them easy access to the pier. Their mute companion pulled himself up onto the dock, gesturing for Doc and Raider to pass him the bundles of cargo.

Doc shook his head, indicating that he was not yet ready to unload the vessel. "We don't know where we're going from here, so I see no need to . . .Raider, what are you—"

The big man nodded toward the uniformed man who strode along the wooden cords of the dock.

"Federale," the big man said.

The soldier carried an old breech-loading, single-shot rifle. He greeted them in broken English. "Señors, what can I ask is the hell that you are doing here?"

Doc unfolded a document and presented it for the soldier. The man read the paper carefully before giving it back to them. Then he slung his rifle over his shoulder and walked away without a word.

Raider sighed. "Reckon we're legal."

Doc had a curious expression on his countenance. "Well, we're here. Now I suppose we should decide what we're going to do next."

Raider chuckled a little. "Yeah, that might just be a good idea. How about gettin' the hell out of this toy boat?"

The pier felt as tentative as the deck of the sloop. Raider hesitated when he hit real ground. His legs stiffened at the feel of land.

Doc glanced around, looking for the soldier. "I wanted to ask that *federale* if he had seen any sign of the liaison officer."

"What the hell was his name, anyway?"

"Sanchez," Doc replied. He looked at the red sky overhead. "It'll be dark soon. We should procure a place to rest for the night and . . . what in God's name?"

"Sounds like a fight," Raider replied.

A screech resounded in the afternoon quiet. Two men tumbled out of a planked shanty, wrestling in the dirt. Raider saw the flashing of steel as the knife was raised high, intended for the chest of the man on the ground.

Raider's next move was purely instinctive. His hand drew the Peacemaker from the holster, thumbing back the hammer. When the Colt exploded, the knife blade broke into two pieces.

The knife-wielding man gawked at Raider with disbelieving eyes.

"Next one is in your chest, hombre."

Even if he had not understood the words, the man had discerned the meaning of the smoking gun barrel. He scurried to his feet and ran down the street away from the Colt. The *federale* appeared again before Raider had the Peacemaker in his holster.

"Geeve me your gun, señor."

Raider stepped back. "Hey, chief, I didn't shoot that boy. I just stopped him from killin' that other one."

"Anh?"

"Shit," the big man said, "I reckon we ain't gonna find nobody around here who talks English."

"Oh, no, señor. I speak the gringo tongue plenty good."

It was the man on the ground, the one whose life had been saved by Raider's Colt. He stepped between Raider and the Mexican soldier, talking a blue streak in Spanish. The soldier eyed them warily for a moment and then nodded. He started to walk away, but Doc stopped him.

The man from Boston turned to their interpreter. "Ask him if he has seen a man named Sanchez, an officer of the government."

The question was relayed, the answer given. "No, señor. He has not seen nobody like that."

"Very well."

The soldier walked away, keeping one eye over his shoulder.

"I don't think he likes you too much, señor."

Doc regarded the man for the first time. He was short but solidly built, carrying himself with a posture that differed greatly from the other inhabitants of the waterfront. Loose-fitting shirt and trousers, homemade sandals, a dark beard, and a bandanna tied around his head like a pirate.

Doc extended his hand to him. "Thank you, sir, for assisting us."

The man laughed. "It is I who should say *gracias*. That loco hombre was going to stab me. If you had not helped I would now be dead."

"Forget it," Raider replied. "Doc, we better find someplace to sleep. It's gonna be dark soon."

The Mexican man raised his hands. "I can help you, señor. I am Poncho."

Raider frowned at the eager servant. "We don't need no help."

"Raider," Doc said, "we could use a guide in these parts. After all, we aren't exactly familiar with this territory."

"*Sí!*" Poncho cried. "I am knowing plenty here. I can take you anywhere. And I don't want many pesos. You can pay me what you wish."

Doc raised an eyebrow. "Five pesos a day."

Poncho frowned comically. "That's all?"

"Ten?"

"Si, señor. I will guide you plenty good."

Raider squinted at the lengthening shadows. "How about guidin' us to a place where we can siesta?"

Poncho clapped his hands together. "Yes, I know a clean, dry shack on the river."

Before he could start forward, Doc put a hand on his shoulder. "We'll have to secure our boat as well. And I will need some information."

Poncho's brow wrinkled.

"I will need to talk to some of the local residents, preferably one or two of the older people, someone who might remember things that happened close to fifty years ago."

Their Mexican guide nodded. *"Sí,* but that is a very long time."

Raider scoffed. "Well, if you can't do it, Poncho . . ."

Poncho stiffened proudly. "There is nothing that I cannot do, señor. Now, if you will follow me."

"Our boat?" Doc asked.

"Pull it along, señor. We will walk along the riverbank."

With that, Poncho scurried ahead of them. Doc motioned for the deaf-mute to come along. They followed after Poncho, who seemed to know his way around the waterfront.

"Speaks English pretty good," Raider offered.

"Too good," Doc replied.

Raider didn't like the tone of his partner's voice. "You on to somethin' I ought to know?"

"No. I suppose I'm being overly cautious in a foreign place."

Raider chortled. "What's that you're always sayin' about doin' what it takes to get along in a strange place."

"When in Rome, do as the Romans do."

"That's it."

"We're not in Rome, Raider."

A far-off cry resounded from the water, reverberating up the shores of the river.

"No, Doc," the big man replied, "I guess we ain't in Rome. I guess we ain't at that."

• • •

Poncho found them a dry hut with a thatched roof and corn-shuck mattresses. Their new associate insisted on unloading the dinghy to store Doc's equipment in the hut. With the help of the deaf-mute, the gear was secured in half an hour. Poncho smiled and bowed to Doc, saying that he would return in the morning, hopefully with information that might be helpful to their investigation.

When Poncho was gone, Raider leaned back on one of the mattresses, rubbing his gun with an oil cloth. "He's awful obligin'."

Doc's hands were busy on the wick of a coal-oil lamp. "You sound as if you don't trust him."

"I reckon I did save his life." He sighed. "Shit, Doc, what are we gonna root up down here? Sittin' in the middle of goddarn nowhere on some wild goose chase."

The lantern flickered to life. Doc torched a cheroot on the flame and then dropped the glass shield. "I must admit I'm beginning to think we're not going to find much. But that would suit me fine."

Raider thought about the two dead men whose reputations were on the line. "Yeah, I see what you mean." He sat up suddenly. "Hey, where's that deaf kid? Did he leave with Poncho?"

Doc's eyes glowed orange in the lantern light. "Yes. Let's get some sleep, Raider. I have a feeling we're going to need it."

Raider reclined on the corn shucks with his rifle and pistol cradled at his side. He closed his eyes, but the bizarre noises outside the hut kept him awake for a long time. What kind of cat was that howling in the darkness? A cougar from hell? He dreamed of mountain lions until Doc's shouting woke him up.

He ran out onto the riverbank with his rifle in hand. The day was burning hot, even though it wasn't much past dawn. Doc pointed at the water, where the dinghy had been.

"Gone!"

Raider levered the Winchester. "That Mex got us."

Doc looked to both sides. "I don't see our mute friend."

Raider tried to take a deep breath. "All right, we been

pinched. But it won't do us any good to sit around and cry."

Doc nodded. "You stay here with the equipment. I'll make inquiries."

"By yourself?"

"Raider, we need to avoid pilferage of—"

A voice rolled over the water. Doc turned back toward the deep, black flow of the Panuco River. Two long wooden canoes cut through the swirling current. A man was waving from the lead vessel.

"Señor! It is me, Poncho!"

The mute poled the canoe behind the Mexican man.

Raider lowered the barrel of the Winchester. "Keep it comin', Poncho."

Their guide laughed. "Señor, you would not shoot me, I'm too valuable to you." He steered the canoe into shore, smiling up at the big cowboy.

Raider scowled at him. "What'd you do with our boat, boy?"

"I traded it," Poncho replied. "Señor, you do not want to go upriver in that small boat. The alligators would eat you."

Doc examined the canoes and then nodded approvingly. "They must be fifteen feet long. Plenty of room for our cargo." He fixed his gaze on Poncho. "But did I hear you say we're going upriver?"

"Sí! I have heard of a man who may help you. He lives inland, near Valles. He is a very old man, a mestizo."

Raider grimaced. "That some kinda medicine man or somethin'?"

Poncho laughed. "No, señor, it means he is mixed blood. Spanish and Indian. Some say he is part Huastec, from very long ago. But this cannot be sure. Sometimes the Indians here say things that are not true, only fables."

Doc slipped off his coat, loosening his collar in the heat. "Poncho, can you find this old man?"

"I think so."

Doc turned to his partner. "Shall we try it?"

Raider shrugged and then glared at Poncho. "This better not be some kinda ambush."

The Mexican man stiffened proudly. "Señor, if you do not

want me to help you, then find someone else."

"Aw, now, don't go featherin' up like a damned banty rooster."

Doc nodded at Poncho. "We'd prefer to get under way at once."

Poncho smiled again. "*Si, señor.* My friend here will help me load the canoes. Does not speak or hear, but he understands enough."

Doc gazed upriver. "How long will it take us to get to Valles?"

Poncho shrugged. "A week, maybe more."

"Ain't you forgettin' somethin', Doc?"

The man from Boston turned to his partner. "I beg your pardon."

"That Sanchez, the man from the government who's supposed to meet us down here. You want to wait for him?"

Doc smiled. "If he were coming, he would be here already. Wouldn't he, Poncho?"

"Huh? Oh, yes, señor, I would have seen him."

"There you have it," Doc replied. "If Mr. Sanchez wants to catch up with us, he will have to follow our trail. Now, if you will excuse me, I'm going to try to find some breakfast."

Raider thought some grub would be a good idea.

Their new associate was way ahead of them. Poncho had brought bananas, cold beans, and tortillas. As he ate, Raider watched Poncho and the deaf lad load the canoes. The trip was going to be a lot easier with two extra men.

The big man wiped his mouth with the back of his hand. "We got to give that deaf boy a name, even if he can't hear it."

Doc swallowed a piece of banana. "Any suggestions?"

"How about Tommy? That's as good as any."

Doc just nodded. He seemed to be keeping his eye on the hardworking pair. Did he have the same suspicions that churned inside his partner? Raider kept asking himself why he felt funny about the way things had fallen into place. He couldn't bring himself to trust the Mexican man and the deaf-mute boy.

A week out of Tampico, however, Raider changed his mind about Poncho and Tommy, mainly because there was a lot you could learn about a man when it came to a head-on fight. It was a lot easier to trust someone if you knew he was willing to risk his life to save you.

The canoes hung in midstream, fixed by the long poles that dug into the river bottom. A shirtless Raider held one pole, while Tommy clung to the staff of the other dugout. Poncho stood in front of the mute, peering toward a fork in the river. Doc was in the bow of Raider's boat, trying to read a rumpled map. Seven days on the black water and they were halted by a simple fork in the road.

"Which way to Valles?" Raider asked.

Doc shook his head. "We'll just have to try one or the other. Poncho, which fork would you take?"

No reply from the Mexican man. His eyes were fixed on the thick growth that rose up between the forks of the stream. Doc went back to the map.

Raider looked up at the sun peaking between the narrow gap between the tropical treetops. Monkeys swung in the branches, chattering away. Poncho had shot one for dinner their third day out of Tampico. Raider wouldn't eat any of it, claiming that he would never bite into something that looked so much like a man.

"Hell, Doc, I ain't been in heat like this since the last time I was in Louisiana."

Doc didn't seem to hear him. The man from Boston, who had abandoned his suit coat and overgaiters, glanced back at Poncho's canoe. "We have to decide. Shall I toss a coin?"

Poncho traced the sign of the Cross over his chest. "It soon will not matter, señor Doc. We will be lucky if live to make the choice."

Three watercraft, log rafts built from thick trees, swung out on the end of the point, sliding effortlessly across the water like Okefenokee cottonmouth moccasins. Seven men in all. Raider couldn't see their faces in the shadows. His hand eased down to his rifle.

"River pirates," Poncho said. "They will want everything we have."

Raider jacked a shell into the chamber of the rifle. "I'm gonna play 'em a little Winchester music."

He fired quickly, popping off two rounds. One of the pirates grabbed his chest, falling over into the river, gushing a slick of blood that caused long, knotty, reptilian tails to slip silently off the riverbank. The pirates dived in next to the blood-hungry alligators.

The rafts drifted back toward the shoreline. Raider scanned the water's surface, but he couldn't make out the fluttering shapes in the ebony current. He leveled his eyes on the other canoe, waiting for some advice from Poncho. But their guide had vanished into the river along with the deaf boy.

Doc was fumbling in a box, searching for his Diamondback. He found the pistol and raised it over the bow of the canoe. The water erupted in front of him. Four arms lifted the canoe, tilting it to the right.

Raider lost his balance, tumbling overboard. Doc held tight to the sides of the dugout, wondering if the pirates were going to tip it over completely. They did not set his mind at ease. The canoe rolled, sending Doc and all of his equipment into the river.

The big man from Arkansas kicked in the effluent, keeping his head above the surface. When he reached a shallow sandbar, he stood up, drawing his rusty Colt from his holster. A musket exploded from the trees, sending a lead ball past his head. Raider fanned the Colt, happy to find that it was in working order. The musket man fell between the broad leaves of a banana tree.

A slosh from behind the big man. One of the pirates shot up on his back like a waterspout. Raider grabbed the wrist with a knife in it. He swung the butt of the Colt backward, crunching the man's ribs. Then he dropped his weight, flinging the man over his back with a move Doc had showed him. He kept the twitching body underwater until it was deathly still. When Raider let go, the corpse floated downstream.

He turned and looked for Doc. Another body floated in the current. Poncho? The deaf boy? Suddenly one of the canoes righted and a dirty-faced river rat poled the vessel straight at Raider.

The big man took aim with the Colt. He fired, but this time he was not so lucky. The cartridge fizzled instead of exploding. A blade gleamed in the hand of the pirate. Raider was going to dive in the river, but he peered down to see an alligator coming straight for him. The big man froze for an instant when he saw the red glow of the 'gator's eyes.

The knife man drew back. Then there was a scream. Someone swung from the trees on a leaf-covered vine. Poncho sailed out over the river, dropping down on the canoe. When the vessel tipped, the knife man joined the alligator in the water.

A pistol sounded to Raider's right. The slug thudded hollowly on the alligator's thick skull. The gator did a death roll in front of the big man. Raider turned toward the riverbank to see the smoking Diamondback in his partner's hand.

"How many are left?" Doc cried.

"Three, maybe—"

A horrific cry came from the branches over Doc's head. A body rolled off the green tangle, thudding into the river. The man had been holding an old army Colt. Another thudding next to Doc. Tommy had jumped down beside him, a bloody knife in his hand.

"Two left now," Raider said.

The canoe righted again. A slippery figure huddled low in the dugout. The knife man? He started to ride the canoe downstream, away from the fracas. Suddenly Poncho was swimming in the current, following the canoe. Doc and Raider watched as Poncho caught the dugout and swung over the side.

The fleeing man turned with a knife, but Poncho was quicker. He diverted the angle of the blade, turning it back into the man's chest. The body fell into the river with the others.

Raider shook his head in disbelief. "I ain't never seen anybody that quick before. You reckon we got all of 'em?"

As if he had heard Raider, the knife man came up out of the river, wielding his blade. Doc fired, but the slug missed him by a good six inches. The man hesitated, marking Raider. He drew back again, only to scream and drop the knife into the stream.

Something twisted in front of the knife man. An alligator had grabbed the soft part of his stomach, spinning around to rip away the flesh. For an instant, the man watched his own entrails as they spilled into the river. Then he was pulled down by the 'gator.

The water was alive with white teeth. Raider thrashed toward the shore where Doc stood with Tommy. He stepped onto the riverbank and held up his Colt.

"Gonna take me a damned year to get it back to shinin'."

Doc nodded toward the river. "Your weapon is the least of our worries. We barely escaped with our lives. Without Poncho and Tommy, we probably wouldn't have stood a chance."

Raider squinted as the Mexican man guided the canoe upstream again. Poncho poled the dugout next to the bank. Raider grabbed the bow and pulled it forward into the dirt.

Poncho looked up at them and smiled. "Pray, my friends, to the blessed Virgin."

Raider grimaced at the clownish guide. "I'd rather thank you, hombre."

Doc suddenly lifted his Diamondback and pointed it at the man in the canoe. "I wouldn't move too much, my friend."

Raider squinted at his partner. "Doc, what the hell!"

Poncho threw up his hands. "Please, señor, I don't know—"

"I want to know who you really are," Doc said firmly. "If you don't tell me, I shall be forced to abandon you right here."

"Doc, he just—"

"I don't care what he did. I want to know the truth about him. If he doesn't comply, then I cannot be responsible for the actions I must take."

Raider peered down at the trembling Poncho, whose eyes were locked with Doc's. After a moment, the big man from Arkansas witnessed a complete change in the Mexican man's posture. Poncho straightened up, standing taller in the canoe. His shoulders stiffened, his head tilted proudly. He tore off the bandanna that covered his head. When he spoke again, the difference in his voice was evident.

"What gave me away, Weatherbee?"

Doc raised an eyebrow. "Oh, you were quite convincing in the beginning. But I began to notice little things. The way you dealt with the *federale*, your efficiency on the journey upriver.

And now this. You certainly don't handle yourself like a ne'er-do-well."

Poncho tipped his hand to the man from Boston. "I refused to believe the stories I had heard about Pinkerton men. Now I must defer to your professionalism."

Raider was frowning. "Somebody wanna tell me what's goin' on?"

Doc seemed to ignore him. "One thing, my friend. Why the act? Couldn't you have approached us directly?"

The Mexican man shrugged. "I had to know if you were honest men. After all, we may find a great deal of wealth when we—"

Raider stepped in front of his partner. "Now you two better let me in on this, before I lose my temper."

Doc gestured toward the man in the canoe. "Unless I miss my guess, we are looking at Colonel Julio Sanchez, Mexican Army."

Sanchez nodded. "That I am. If you will allow me to come ashore, I will shake hands with both of you."

"Hell, why not?" Raider said.

As Sanchez stepped forward, Tommy reached down to steady the bow of the canoe. Raider clapped him on the back and smiled. The boy ignored his efforts to sign "good job."

Sanchez extended his hand to both of them. "I am glad now that the ruse is over. We can speak as equals."

Doc gestured toward the fork in the river. "Are you sure the ruse is over? What are we really heading for up there?"

Sanchez's new accent was less broken. "I told you before, there is an old man upriver. He can tell us many things."

"Then you know about the Alamo and the gold?" Raider asked.

Sanchez nodded. "*Si*. Rather, yes. I was informed by my government. Of course, you can understand how eager General Díaz is to get back the gold that is rightfully ours."

Raider's first urge was to say something about how the Texans had kicked Santa Anna's ass all the way back to Mexico. About how the gold was taken during wartime so it was really the property of the State of Texas. But he refrained, figuring one stubborn Pink was not going to come between two governments that were in agreement.

Doc examined the fork in the river. "The pirates came from the left. Perhaps we should go in that direction."

Sanchez shook his head. "No. If we go left, we will probably find a small tributary that leads to the pirate's hideout. I say we go right."

Doc turned toward his partner. "Raider?"

He thought about it and then said, "Poncho, I mean Sanchez, ain't led us astray so far. I say we trust him until he shows us different."

"A wise choice, Raider," replied the Mexican officer.

Raider pointed a finger at Sanchez. "No more bullshit, though. You shoot straight with us about everything."

Sanchez nodded.

Doc gazed back at the river. His boxes and bundles were floating all over the place. "I suppose we'd better gather up my equipment."

"What about them bodies?" Raider asked.

"The alligators will take care of them," Sanchez replied. "Such men do not deserve to be buried."

Raider looked askance at Sanchez. "You know somethin', Colonel? I'm gettin' to where I almost like you."

"I wish I could say the same about you, señor."

Raider frowned for a moment; a promise of trouble, Doc thought. But then Sanchez laughed and Raider laughed too. They enjoyed a hearty chuckle before they returned to their task on the deep, black waters of the Panuco River.

CHAPTER NINE

As the afternoon shadows grew longer, Raider kept his eyes trained on the dense tropical forest. In his travels as an agent for Allan Pinkerton, the big man had never seen such tangled treetops. Nor had he seen the variety of animals—colorful parrots, parakeets, monkeys, ringtails, and snakes—that stared back at him, unafraid, from the shaggy clumps of vegetation. Each bend of the river forced his hand closer to the rust-molded .45 at his side.

He gazed ahead at Sanchez, who rode in the lead canoe as they wound deeper into the verdant heart of the jungle. "Hey, Julio, are you sure we're on the right track?"

Sanchez waved him off without an answer. Raider grunted at Doc, who sat in front of him in the second dugout. The soggy pearl-gray derby had wilted on Doc's sandy head. The man from Boston seemed to be weathering the journey with his usual resilience. His disposition had improved when they recovered most of his equipment from the river. Raider's own Stetson had floated off to parts unknown.

"Gonna be too dark to go on pretty soon, Doc."

No reply from the gentleman Pinkerton. His eyes were focused on a catlike shape moving through the trees. A jaguar, Sanchez had said, was the most dangerous animal in Mexico.

"Hey, Doc."

"Shh, I think Sanchez is expecting something."

Raider slapped a mosquito that left a blood mark as big as a copper penny on his arm. He'd have to use some more of the sticky substance Sanchez had given them to repel the army of jungle insects. The Mexican officer knew about things like that. He had shown them how to make camp in the dugouts, reclining under a cloth tent to keep snakes from dropping down on them while they were sleeping. He knew the exact plant to use for the rash that had erupted on Raider's neck and shoulders. Now if he could just find the old mestizo man, whose existence Raider was beginning to question.

Sanchez raised his hand and Tommy fixed the wooden pole in the river bottom. The colonel motioned for Doc and Raider to pull alongside. When they were close enough, Sanchez grabbed the bow of their canoe.

"We are very near," the colonel said.

Raider glared at him. "How much longer?"

Sanchez peered up at the sky. "We can go another hour today. If we don't find what we are looking for by then, we will surely come on it tomorrow."

"And if we don't?" Raider challenged.

Sanchez cast his eyes on the ever-darkening roof of the jungle. "Then we will all be trying to find our asses without a gaslight."

Raider had to laugh at that one. "Press on then, Colonel. Just remember that you have two quick-handed Pinks behind you. And both of us are totin' guns."

"I wouldn't want it any other way," Sanchez replied.

Doc was gazing ahead at the bend in the river. "If we don't find this man, I'm afraid we must turn back."

"Afraid of what you might find?" Sanchez asked.

"We're waiting for you to take the lead," Doc replied dryly.

With Tommy at the helm, the dugout moved ahead of them, rounding the overgrown bend. Raider poled their vessel, keeping pace against the current. They followed the river's meandering course, disappointed at each twist and turn. Darkness began to overtake the low-lying areas, prompting Sanchez to stop again in midstream. Raider guided his dugout next to the colonel.

"We must find a place to tie up for the night," Sanchez said. "Perhaps there is a sandbar ahead or a clear piece of bank."

"Why would you think that?" Doc asked.

Sanchez shrugged. "Perhaps my thoughts are full of hope."

Doc could not argue with that assessment. He slapped a mosquito on his neck. Sanchez gave them both some more of the insect potion. It felt cool on their skin. The deaf lad salved himself as well.

Raider pointed toward the narrow stretch of river ahead of them. "One more bend and then we hang it up for the night."

Sanchez nodded. "If I heard the truth in Tampico, we cannot be far from our destination."

Doc's eyes narrowed. "You said yourself that the Indian people sometimes fabricate their own legends."

"Yes," Sanchez replied. "That is exactly what I said."

He gestured with his right hand, prompting Tommy to move them forward. Raider's arms strained as he made the effort to follow. The jungle was starting to look damned spooky in the dark. The forest hadn't been as thick downriver. Now it seemed to be hanging over them with skinny fingers of green. Then they turned the bend and suddenly the riverbank was alive with glowing torches and eerie faces that peered out at them from a strange light.

The torches illuminated a thatched hut in a small clearing. Raider counted five bodies in the circles of light. Their faces were painted with some sort of white wash. His hand dropped to the butt of his Peacemaker.

"I could plug 'em now," the big man said.

"No!" Sanchez replied. "Look closely. They are women."

Raider squinted, perceiving the fatty bulges on their bare chests. "Son of a bitch if they ain't. Only, women know how to kill too."

"Steady," Doc replied. "Allow the colonel to speak to them diplomatically before you get carried away."

Sanchez stood up in the canoe, holding out his arms. He called something in a language that did not sound like Spanish. No response from the shore.

"That don't sound like no Mex-talk I ever heard," Raider said.

"They don't speak Spanish," Sanchez replied. "At least not the same language that I learned to speak in Mexico City."

He called again in a blend of Spanish and an Indian dialect. One of the women picked up a torch and waved it at them. Sanchez sat down again.

"All right, Mr. Weatherbee. We have been invited ashore. Raider, you will have to leave your weapons in the canoe."

The big man grimaced. "And trust these jungle people?"

"If we must," Sanchez replied. "These are the old man's daughters and wives. No harm will come to us if we mind our manners."

"Do your hear that?" Doc rejoined. "Even in the jungle you must learn to be polite, Raider."

The big man surrendered to their directive, not bothering to tell them that he had a knife in his boot. You never went into a strange encampment without some form of backup. He pushed his canoe onto the sandy bank, next to Sanchez's vessel. The women grabbed the bows of the dugouts, pulling them safely onto shore.

"Thank you," Doc said, bowing to the ladies.

But they did not meet his gaze. Rather, they eyed his boxes of equipment, as if a treasure had been brought into their camp. Sanchez gestured to Tommy, telling him that he should stay with the canoes. The deaf boy nodded, his face alive with fear in the torchlight.

Raider saluted him. "Reckon he wouldna come along if he knowed it was gonna be this bad."

Suddenly three women were standing in front of the big man. They took his arms and started to lead him toward the thatched hut. Doc and Sanchez fell in behind the procession. The women were muttering some low, haunting incantation.

"What's this about?" Doc asked.

"I'm not sure," Sanchez replied. "They seem to think Raider is some sort of holy man."

Doc gave a disapproving grunt. "There doesn't seem to be any accounting for good judgment, even in the jungle."

The trio of women stopped at the entrance to the hut. They pulled back a piece of tattered cloth that covered the threshold. Raider looked over his shoulder at Doc and Sanchez. The colonel urged him forward. All three of them entered the musky-smelling confines of the primitive dwelling.

The light was dim inside the hut. They heard the heavy breathing of a man in poor health. A bony hand stretched out toward them from a pallet on the sandy floor. Sanchez barely understood the words uttered by the shriveled old man.

"He is sick," Sanchez said. "He says a holy man will come to help him. His daughters told him of this."

Doc knelt beside the withered body. He felt the man's forehead, which was feverish. He asked Sanchez to get the man to describe his symptoms. The voice was barely audible as the man muttered his ailments to the colonel.

"He is hot all over. His stomach hurts him. He says he ate some bad meat and now the gods are punishing him."

"Which gods?" Raider asked skeptically.

Sanchez warded him off with a stern stare. "Do not make fun of their deities, señor. Their faith is strong."

Doc's fingers touched the old man's stomach for a moment. "I don't know if I can cure him, but I can certainly mix the appropriate powders."

Doc stood up, but Raider put a hand on his shoulder. "Hold it, Weatherbee." The big man looked at Sanchez. "Tell him the holy man will treat him, but he's gotta tell us what we want to know after that."

Sanchez glared at Raider through slitted eyes. "Sometimes you can be very cruel, señor."

"Tell him!"

Sanchez extracted the promise from the old man. Doc hurried back to the canoes, where the women still eyed his possessions. He retrieved the appropriate chemicals from his medical bag, mixing the formula for a simple physic to counteract a sour stomach and a fever.

When he was inside the hut again, he had trouble convincing the old man to swallow the medicine. Holy men, it seemed, did not bring cures in a cup, but rather healed instantly with their great powers. Finally Sanchez made the old man believe that the great powers were concentrated in the bubbling liquid. As soon as he had swallowed the elixir, the old man dropped off into a deep sleep.

Raider shook his head. "Looks like we're gonna have to wait awhile. Hell, at least we found him. Good job, Sanchez."

The colonel was frowning. "I hope he does not die."

"He is old," Doc replied. "He may pass on from natural causes."

"You do not understand," Sanchez said. "If he has daughters, he may have sons. They could be hunting in the jungle, or they could have fled when they saw us coming. I would not want to be traveling on this river with a band of vengeful Indians chasing us."

He had a point, Raider thought. The old man groaned in his sleep. The hairs on Raider's neck suddenly stood at attention. He hunkered down next to Doc and kept his eyes on the ancient mestizo gentleman, praying to God that he would awake in the morning.

The old man's chest rattled, a dreadful sound of air being forced from his lungs. Raider, who had been dozing, opened his eyes. He nudged Doc and Sanchez, who had slept sitting next to him. Doc hovered over the old man, feeling his forehead.

"The fever has broken," Doc said.

The old man gestured for Doc to help him to his feet. When he was upright, he staggered outside his hut and vomited profusely into the sand. For a moment, Doc thought he was going to fall down. But the old man only lifted his arms in triumph, drawing cheers from his wives and daughters. He turned back toward Doc and Raider, smiling as he mumbled a few words.

Sanchez laughed. "He says he is a very special old man. His name is One Who Cheats the Condors."

"What's a condor?" Raider asked.

"A vulture," Sanchez replied.

Doc was smiling now. "Tell him he certainly lived up to his name."

The colonel's brow wrinkled. "I must ask him what we need to know."

Sanchez urged the old man inside the hut. The daughters brought a wooden platter full of bananas and papayas. As the condor cheater stuffed his toothless mouth, he slurred something to Sanchez.

"He says to never eat meat," the colonel said. "He says the gods do not approve and will try to take you if you do."

Raider chortled at the old man. "Probably chawin' down on some of that monkey meat."

The big man found that he was hungry, so he helped himself to the platter of fruit. Sanchez and Doc ate their fill as well. When they had finished, the old man produced a wooden pipe from beneath his pallet. He stuffed the bowl with a greenish substance and then bade one of his daughters to bring him a coal from the fire outside.

Doc surprised the old gentleman by producing a sulphur match and striking it off his thumbnail. The condor cheater hesitated for a moment before he lowered his pipe to the flame. He puffed a few times and offered the pipe to the trio of men who sat in front of him. They all smoked, not wanting to offend their host.

Raider suddenly felt light-headed. "Must be some of that locoweed."

"Cannabis," Doc replied.

The old man started to laugh. He muttered something to Sanchez, who passed the pipe back to him. The condor cheater filled his lungs again. A vacant smile twisted his toothless mouth.

"He hears the music," Sanchez said.

Raider tried to focus his eyes. "I can hear a banjo myself."

Doc, who had not inhaled the smoke, urged Sanchez to inquire after their purpose. For a long time the colonel bantered with the old man, whose memory was good but unpointed. He could recall things from way back, but often the dialogue would dwindle into laughter or an indistinguishable dialect.

"He cannot remember," Sanchez said. "I think he is too old."

Raider scowled at the colonel. "He's got to remember."

Doc had his fist on his chin. "Julio, ask him about the two white men who may have come this way. Ask him about the men with much gold. Did they run away from here?"

Sanchez went through a tedious combination of words and gestures, trying to jog the old man's memory. Finally the condor cheater's clotted eyes gleamed in the shadows of the hut. He shook his head, drawing on the pipe. His story lasted a while, and Sanchez could only understand part of it.

"Two men passed this way, but he does not remember how long ago. He was still young then, but not a boy. They were carrying a trunk—he remembers because he tried to touch it and they would not let him."

Doc nodded. "Now we're getting somewhere. Ask him if he remembers which way they went."

Again they played the game of language and signing. The old man seemed to get carried away by the tale. He even stood up, gesturing to the west and calling out a word that they all understood.

"Zacatecas. Zah-kah-tay-kas." He seemed proud of his pronunciation.

Sanchez urged the old man to lie down.

"What's he sayin'?" Raider asked.

"The men went west," Sanchez replied. "To a region known as Zacatecas. He helped them most of the way. His brothers were alive then. They paid them in gold."

Doc asked if the old man still had any of the gold. The reply came that the gold had long since been spent. The old man could not remember if the gold coins looked like the one found in Hollis Morton's strongbox.

Raider leaned back, still under the influence of the pipe. "Shit, Doc, this old geezer could be talkin' out of his ass. And if he ain't, how many fortune hunters passed this way? It coulda been anybody."

Doc looked at Sanchez. "Ask him if he can describe the men."

After another dialogue session, Sanchez shook his head. "They passed so long ago that he does not remember."

The condor cheater said something else that made Sanchez open his eyes much wider.

"He says he does have something that was given to him by one of them."

"Ask him if we can see it," Doc said.

When Sanchez relayed the request, the old man called for

one of his daughters. He made the girl fetch something from a secret hiding place. She returned with a leather pouch. The old man held it out for Doc, the holy man who had saved him.

"Thank you, sir."

Doc opened the worn flap on the leather pouch. He felt something furry when he reached into the bag. When he pulled it out, Raider choked on a breath of air. The fur had become brittle over the years, but it was still evident to the big man that Doc was holding a coonskin hat in his hands.

"I gotta get outta here," Raider said, crawling through the doorway.

Doc put the coonskin hat back in the leather bag. He gave it to the old man and then excused himself, following his partner. Sanchez stayed with the condor cheater for a few minutes and then made his excuses to the mestizo, charging angrily out of the hut toward Doc and Raider.

"How dare you insult the old man like that!" the colonel cried. "You are lucky that I could keep him from being offended."

Raider swung a hard right hand into Sanchez's jaw, knocking the officer to the ground. Sanchez stayed down, not wanting to challenge the bigger man. Raider turned away, ashamed of himself for unloading on an ally.

Doc reached down to help the colonel to his feet. "I must apologize for my partner, Colonel Sanchez. However, I can almost understand his loss of temper. I must admit I am a bit nonplussed."

Sanchez rubbed his jaw. "How can you defend him for being—"

Raider wheeled toward Sanchez. "Davy Crockett wore a coonskin cap, Colonel. You savvy?"

"And they paid the old man in gold," Doc added.

Sanchez's face lit up. "Then we're on the right path."

"As far as we can see," Doc replied.

"Damn it all to hell!" Raider grumbled.

The old man's voice resounded behind them. He was caterwauling, chanting the same cadence over and over. His crooked finger pointed toward the west.

Raider didn't like the tenor of the man's tone. "What's he sayin'?"

Sanchez listened for a moment and then said, "He's telling us to go west, to the land of the smoking mountain."

The big man from Arkansas frowned at the interpretation. "What the hell does that mean?"

"Zacatecas," Sanchez replied. "I will show you on the map. We must follow the river as far as we can, and then we will travel by foot."

"No horses?" Doc asked.

Sanchez shook his head. "Where we are going, señor, you cannot take a horse." He started for the canoes.

Raider grabbed the colonel's shoulder. "Sorry about the fist, Julio. I didn't rightly know what I was doin'. That locoweed's got me crazy."

Sanchez shrugged away from Raider's grasp. "It does not matter, señor."

"No, I mean it."

"Hear me," Sanchez rejoined. "In Tampico, when I was fighting with the man who had the knife, I was not acting. The fight was real. You saved my life then, señor, so your hitting me squares the debt. I do not owe you now."

Raider deferred to the colonel's sense of honor. "If that's the way you see it, I ain't gonna argue."

"You'd better not hit me again, señor."

Sanchez turned away and walked toward the canoes.

Doc grinned at his partner. "I think he means it, Raider."

The old man was still laughing and talking.

Land of the smoking mountain. Raider wasn't sure he liked the sound of that. Land of the smoking mountain. And that damned coonskin hat!

Raider stood in the rear of the canoe, his black eyes fixed on an impenetrable wall of green. "Where the hell did the river go, Sanchez?"

The colonel shook his head. "The flow ends here. There is a swamp beyond. The river is fed by the swamp and the mountains."

The big man scratched the three-week growth of beard on his face. "I don't see no mountains."

"They are on the other side of this jungle," Sanchez replied.

Doc, whose face had sprouted a sandy growth, stood up, peering into the dense verdure. "We can't navigate these canoes through that—that forest. We'll have to chop our way through."

"Precisely, Señor Weatherbee. I have machetes."

Doc took off the bandanna that had replaced the pearl-gray derby on his head. His shirt was also torn and ragged, his fine tricot pants a memory. He looked down at the two boys who sat in the bottom of the canoe. The condor cheater's sons had come out of the jungle in time to travel upriver with them. Now the young men were looking nervous. One of them spoke to Sanchez in a high voice.

Sanchez listened and then translated for Doc and Raider. "They will not go on with us. Give them your canoe. They will go back to their encampment."

Raider grunted. "Son of a bitch. Ride another week on this river and we reach a dead end."

"What about my equipment?" Doc asked.

Sanchez shrugged. "We can carry some of it. The rest we must leave behind. I know you do not like it, señor, but if we are to go on, we cannot be burdened by things we don't need."

Doc grumbled, but at last he could not fight logic. He sifted through his belongings, taking his telescope, his pistol, maps, matches, some cooking utensils, and several sticks of dynamite.

Raider eyed the red shafts of explosive. "That stuff's sweatin', Doc. You sure you want to take it along?"

Doc set his medical bag on top of the dynamite. "At this point I'm not sure about anything."

Raider watched as Sanchez and Tommy eased over the side of the lead canoe. They waded toward the jungle, holding long-bladed knives that were a dull iron color. Raider hoisted his gunbelt and his rifle over his shoulder. He took a deep breath and looked down at the condor cheater's offspring. The boys were chattering and pointing into the jungle.

"I wonder what's wrong with them?" the big man said.

Sanchez had heard him. He looked over his shoulder. "They are saying that no one has ever come out of this jungle alive."

Raider had to laugh at that one. "I reckon things could be worse."

"How?" Doc replied.

They joined their comrades in the river, wading toward the forest. As they entered the trees, Raider took one last look at the old man's sons, who were lashing the canoes together. The expression of relief was evident in their dark eyes. He waved, but the boys did not wave back.

"Maybe they think we're already dead."

Sanchez handed him a machete. "You will need this, Señor Raider."

The big man gazed up at the matted vegetation. "How far do we have to go in this mess?"

"I do not know," Sanchez replied. "I have only seen this forest from the other side."

Doc eyed the colonel. "Then you're certain there is another side?"

Sanchez turned and started to hack his way through the vines. "It does not matter, Señor Weatherbee. We have come too far to turn back."

Raider stepped into a watery hole only to feel something slithering from beneath his feet. He grimaced and raised his machete, hacking at the leaves and branches. They earned every foot of the way, cutting a path through the forest, slicing with the knives until their arms ached.

That night they slept in trees, surrounded by the glowing eyes and night sounds of strange animals. When Raider awoke at dawn, he found a small monkey sleeping on his chest. He tried to shoo it away, but the white-faced primate clung tightly to his shoulder, as if he were its father.

"You have found a friend, señor," Sanchez said.

Doc laughed. "Birds of a feather, eh?"

"Hell," Raider grunted. "If he wants to come along, I ain't got enough gumption to tell him no."

They slipped down out of the trees, back to the floor of the forest. Sanchez pointed out which fruits were safe to eat. As he peeled a banana, Doc remarked that they were in some sort of Garden of Eden, but no one took his comparison seriously. Tommy swung down on a vine, landing next to the man from

Boston. He took a banana from Doc's hand, popping it into his mouth.

Raider lifted his machete, striking the first blow of many. They began to plod through the jungle that refused to let up. When the rain started to fall, no one said a word. It was as if the forest had swallowed them up and digested their spirits at the same time. Only the monkey chattered as he rested on the big man's shoulders. He could have been telling them to turn back, an unintelligible warning.

But Doc and Raider were not used to failure. Nor was Sanchez, the pride of General Díaz and the Mexican Army. They swung their blades into the belly of the jungle, obsessed with their task, fighting diligently through the endless wall of green.

CHAPTER TEN

The wide-eyed monkey began to chatter hysterically on Raider's shoulder. The big man from Arkansas looked up, wondering if he could believe his jungle-sharpened senses. Six days in the rain forest had turned all of them into keen-witted animals—less and more than human, depending on the need.

Doc and Sanchez stopped behind Raider, gazing around his broad torso. Their bodies were covered with a green, caked-on lotion that Sanchez had whipped up from the pulp of a jungle tree. It kept the mosquitoes off them as they hacked through the leaves and vines.

Tommy stepped past them and peered at the steep upward slope of the ground in front of them. He could not believe it either. The jungle had been thinning all day, but now they were faced with an incline of dry, solid earth. And a patch of blue sky beyond that!

Sanchez clapped Doc on the back. "We are finished with the jungle for the time being."

The man from Boston looked as if he had been defeated by the forest. "As you say, Colonel."

The monkey continued to dance on Raider's shoulder, clinging to his neck. "Hush up, boy." Raider turned back toward the incline. "I think he smells water. Fresh water. Ain't but one thing to do. Climb!"

Raider's big strides carried him across the soft carpet of mire that bordered the jungle and the uplands. Tommy was right beside him, eager to be out of the forest as well. They paused at the base of the slope, measuring the angle. It was steep, but there seemed to be plenty of handholds in the way of small shrubs and protruding roots.

"Looks like somebody dug it out here," Raider called back to Doc.

The gentleman Pinkerton did not reply.

"Anyway, here goes."

As Raider climbed the first few feet, Tommy scurried past him. The deaf boy reached the summit quickly, gazing back down to watch Raider as he lifted himself. The monkey was barking incessantly as the big man claimed the slope inch by inch. He hesitated about halfway up the twenty-foot wall.

"Are you going to make it?" Sanchez called from below.

Raider grunted. "Yeah. I just wish this damned ape wasn't singin' in my ear." He lifted his eyes for a moment. Tommy was leaning over the cilff, offering a hand up for the big man. Raider started to climb again, working his way toward the boy's outstretched fingers.

"Not too much further," he whispered to the monkey. "If you can just hang on until we—ow, damn it!"

The monkey had bit him and leapt from his neck, screaming as it flipped down the slope. When it hit the ground it dived onto the trunk of a banana tree. Its frantic chattering resounded through the forest.

Raider squinted up at Tommy. "What the hell was that?"

Then he felt it, a quaking through the earth. Or was it his own muscles losing strength? No, the trembling was in the ground: the entire area had started to shake violently. Tommy had to withdraw his hand and dive for safety.

Raider gripped a root, his hands turning white with the effort to hang on. As the trembling peaked, the root gave way, sliding out of the ground like an unbarbed Indian arrow. Raider fell back toward the earth. His feet hit the soft bed of the jungle and sank in to the ankle. The landscape shook for another ten seconds, rooting the big man in the mire. He felt himself trembling even after the quake had subsided.

Doc and Sanchez pushed apart when they realized they had

been holding on to one another. For a moment they stared at Raider, who seemed to be anchored like a statue. The big man grimaced. "Don't just stand there, you tinhorns. Pull me out of this muck!"

They both regained their senses, stepping forward to free Raider's legs from the mud.

"Reckon we just had us a' earthquake, Weatherbee."

Doc nodded, still keeping quiet. He turned his eyes upward, searching for Tommy on the ledge above them. He gave a sigh of relief when he saw the deaf boy waving back.

Sanchez started forward. "We must climb quickly."

Doc grabbed his shoulder. "A moment. Sometimes there are—"

A less forceful aftershock came and went. They held their breaths until the last vibration had subsided. When the second quake was gone, Raider wasted no time scaling the slope.

At the top, Tommy immediately grabbed his arm and turned him due west for a survey of the topography. Raider gawked at the mountains that rose up in the distance against a blue sky. He felt his stomach churning.

"Doc! Sanchez? You better get up here."

The man from Boston called from below. "What is it?"

Raider could not find the words. "Just get up here."

His black eyes were frozen on the peak of the highest mountain in the group. Tommy saw it too. Emanating from the summit of the mountain was a lazy billowing of dark smoke that curled in circular patterns into the afternoon breeze. He continued to watch until Doc and Sanchez were standing next to him.

"Zacatecas," Sanchez said. "Land of the smoking mountain."

"Of course," Doc replied. "A volcano."

Raider wasn't sure he liked the sound of that word. *Volcano*. He preferred "land of the smoking mountain." Even if the old man's chant still echoed in his mind.

From the edge of the jungle they took a narrow path that led them by late afternoon to the base of the smoking mountain. Doc spied the steam of the hot springs. He had been searching for a miracle with his spyglass. When he declaimed

Divine intervention, Raider squawked that Doc could find a bath in the Mojave Desert if you set it down within a hundred miles of him.

But even the big man had to admit that the warm water felt good. They all soaked for a long time, using the bar of soap Doc had stashed in his pack. He also his had telescope, a single map, a compass, and the three sweaty sticks of dynamite. His fine wardrobe had been reduced to a pair of cutoff trousers, a sleeveless shirt, a pair of makeshift sandals, and a blue bandanna in place of his derby. He looked the worse for wear.

Raider had his rust-flecked Colt, a hunting knife, and a cutoff pair of denim pants. He had stepped out of his boots somewhere in the jungle and had been barefoot ever since. He had refused the jury-rigged sandals offered by Sanchez.

The Mexican man seemed to be holding up best of all. His strength was steady and seemingly limitless. Raider guessed he was more used to the climate. Why the hell did Sanchez keep lifting his eyes to the purple slopes of the mountain? He didn't appear to be lost, but rather to be looking for a landmark to right himself in a familiar place.

Raider wondered if Doc noticed the colonel's roving eyes. The hot bath made Weatherbee *look* like his old self, but had the jungle taken too much out of the city-bred Pinkerton?

Suddenly Doc snapped to attention and regarded the colonel. "Sanchez, you've been studying the area quite closely. I'd like to know what you're looking for."

Raider smiled. Doc was back. He had puffed up like a rooster in a fighting frenzy. He pressed the Mexican man for an answer.

Sanchez finally nodded and gave in. "I have been in this region before, Señor Weatherbee, when I was much younger. Only, I was on the other side of this mountain. And I never got within ten miles of these slopes. We started back the other way."

Raider looked at Sanchez, his eyes narrowed. "We?"

"My company. You see, we were looking for the same gold then."

"Why the hell didn't you find it?" Raider bellowed.

"Our commanding officer was killed," Sanchez replied. "I

was just a soldier then. I remember that his throat was slit. I was the one who found him. We left quickly after he was buried."

Doc looked back up at the mountain. "So you're braving this volcano to settle an old army score?"

"Partly," Sanchez replied. He also lifted his eyes to the peak. "Totonac, it is called. A demon."

"Yes," Doc said, "an erupting volcano is rivaled by few other destructive forces of nature. Ask the citizens of Pompeii."

Raider scowled at his partner. "Pompeii?"

"An ancient city," Doc replied. "It was covered over with fire and lava by Mount Vesuvius. The end of the world, as it were." He looked at Sanchez. "What is on the other side of Totonac, Colonel?"

"The Pyramid of the Sun," Sanchez replied. "A tribe of Indians tends the shrine. Or so legend has it. No one has ever come back from this region."

"You did," Raider said accusingly.

Sanchez shrugged. "We pulled back before there was any more trouble. General Díaz recalled us to Mexico City."

"So you knew about the gold way back when?" Raider asked.

"Yes," Sanchez replied. "Only our legends say the Totonac Indians took it for their own purposes. I must admit that your story makes more sense. The Totonacs never ventured more than five miles from this mountain."

Raider spun the cylinder of his Colt. "Hell, we ain't got enough firepower to stop nothin', much less a whole tribe of Injuns. What if they . . . Jesus, what the hell was that?"

A high-pitched squealing sounded from behind them.

Doc looked around him. "Where's Tommy?"

Raider wheeled to his right, aiming the Colt at the round shape that bolted into the open, running straight for him. The animal raised its pointed snout, showing a few stumpy teeth. Raider squeezed off a shot that caught the hoggish creature between the eyes. It fell squirming onto the ground.

Tommy ran up behind the animal, clapping his hands at Raider's deadly accuracy.

The big man squinted at the carcass. "What the hell is that thing?"

"A tapir," Sanchez replied. "It must come here to drink and feed. I suppose we are close enough to the jungle. You did right shooting it. We'll have meat tonight and then climb Totonac in the morning."

Raider scowled at the colonel. "It ain't a monkey, is it?"

"No, señor."

"Then I'll eat some of it."

Tommy had opened up the tapir's stomach with his knife. As the entrails flowed onto the ground, the mountian rumbled overhead. Smoke continued to swirl into the sky. A fire on the mountain. Raider suddenly tried to remember why they had come to Mexico.

"Pompeii," he muttered under his breath.

Doc turned to his partner. "What did you say?"

Raider shrugged. "I was just thinkin'. You said that volcano thing busted up Pompeii. No survivors."

"Well, the devastation was fairly complete."

"No prisoners at the Alamo either, Doc."

The man from Boston shook his head. "I don't see the similarity."

"I ain't sure I do." He thought for a moment and then said, "Doc, you reckon Jim Bowie and Davy Crockett are up there on that mountain, tellin' us to mind our own business?"

"No," Doc replied. "I don't think that at all."

They built a fire to cook the meat. It tasted wild and strong, but Raider had eaten worse. When his belly was full, he found a flat spot and stretched out to sleep. As the sun descended, the red glow became more apparent over the volcano's peak. A fire *in* the mountain, Raider thought. And they were practically roasting on the Devil's barbecue spit.

The trip up Totonac was unexpectedly easy. A path had been cut in the stone, winding up toward the mouth of the crater like a thinly sliced apple peeling. Somebody had taken a lot of time to carve the trail. And from the looks of things, it had been well traveled. Raider tried to keep his Colt in his hands at all times. He had to wedge it in his belt when he saw the rope ladder at the end of the path.

The big man shook his head. "It's like they want us to find them."

Sanchez replied, "They do not expect someone to come through the jungle."

Tommy jumped up and clung to the rope, testing its strength.

Raider gestured for him to get down. The big man put his foot on the first rung. He was going to say something about what to do if he didn't come back, but then the woman screamed.

They weren't sure they had heard her. Then the voice resounded again, high and shrill and full of terror. It was coming from above them. Raider started up the ladder toward the cries that were now muffled by a hand.

When he peeked over the edge of the crater, he saw a man standing near the volcano's opening. The man was dressed in a feathered suit, an Indian costume; he was probably some kind of medicine man. He had his hands around the throat of a young woman who struggled to be free of him.

"Whoa, Jasper!" Raider cried. "Let her go."

The man released his grip and backed away from the girl. His dark eyes were glaring at Raider. He chanted something and drew a knife. The blade flew straight for the big man, who leaned out of the knife's path. He brought the Colt out of his belt, aiming for a second before he opened up a hole in the medicine man's feathered chest. The high priest of the smoking mountian stumbled forward and fell dead. The woman cried out and fell to the ground as well.

Raider eased himself over the ledge, onto the rim of the crater. He bent over the woman to see that she had simply fainted. Doc came behind him and confirmed his diagnosis.

The smoke had subsided a little. Doc had been feeling tremors all morning, small vibrations in the path. What sort of pressure was building in the earth's boiler room? He didn't know enough about volcanic disturbances to make a conjecture.

"Señor Weatherbee! Look at this!"

Sanchez strode toward the man from Boston, holding something in his hand. A pendant dangled from the colonel's fingers. Doc picked up the medallion and examined it closely. It was old but still recognizable.

"Raider, have a look."

The big man squinted at the coin on the end of the gold chain. "It's Mex all right. Just like the one you found in Morton's strongbox. Where'd you find it, Julio?"

"On the priest. He was wearing it around his neck."

Raider looked at the body. "Is he Totonac?"

"Yes," Sanchez replied. "But the girl is Tiaxcalans. I believe that is how you say it."

"Where did he come from?" Doc asked.

Sanchez strode toward the opposite edge of the crater. "From there, Señor Weatherbee. The Pyramid of the Sun."

Doc and Raider joined the colonel, looking down into an idyllic valley. Below them stretched a dry forest with grass-green patches and flowering gardens between the trees. At the center of the village sat a greenish pyramidal structure that must have been three stories tall.

Doc extended his telescope for a long look. "Remarkable. Did they build that structure? The Totonacs, I mean."

"No," Sanchez replied. "It was built by the ancients."

"What ancients?" Raider asked.

"Does it matter, señor?"

They heard scuffling behind them. Raider glanced back to see Tommy helping the girl to her feet. She ran to Raider as soon as she had regained her balance. Her arms wrapped around his neck, and she thanked him in a language that even Sanchez did not understand.

Raider nodded at the colonel. "What the hell was they doin' up here, anyway? Ain't this a dangerous place to bring a woman?"

"Not if you're going to throw her in," Sanchez replied.

Doc raised an eyebrow. "Sacrifice?"

Sanchez nodded. "She is pure. They are offering her to the gods of the volcano."

"How come they didn't take somebody from their own tribe?" Raider asked.

"Perhaps they did not have someone who was pure."

Doc lifted the gold coin. "Our men, whoever they may be, came this way. I never thought . . ." His jaw clenched. "We've killed their priest, gentlemen. They'll know we are here when he does not come back. There might even be an escort below."

"Maybe they'll think the volcano gods ate him up," Raider offered. "I mean, hell, if they think they can stop this mountain from smokin' by feedin' it a pretty girl . . ."

Raider stroked the woman's fine black hair. She snuggled close to him, whimpering softly. What kind of savage tribe would kill a young woman?

Doc looked over the edge of the crater to see a rope ladder leading down to another path below. He thought he saw movement in the rocks at the base of the ladder. Raider went down despite his partner's warning.

When his foot hit the rocks, two men sprang from hiding and started running along the descending path. Raider took aim and killed one of them immediately. He did not cry out when he fell. The other man managed to escape, although he slipped and lost his balance a few yards down the trail. He also kept silent as he tumbled to his death.

Raider sounded the all-clear for Doc, Sanchez, and Tommy. When they had joined him, he gestured toward the valley. "They know we're here."

Doc straightened his telescope and studied the landscape below. "That should make it easier for us to find them."

"They will find us, Señor Weatherbee." Sanchez smiled. "I suggest we find a place to hide for the night. It will be dark soon. We spent the entire day on this mountain. We can deal with the Totonac in the morning."

Raider gazed back up at the crater. "What about the girl?"

Sanchez gestured to Tommy. "He can go get her."

The deaf lad went up the rope but came back empty-handed.

"She is no longer there," Sanchez said.

Raider snorted at the colonel. "She couldna just disappeared into thin air. I'm gonna have a look for myself."

Raider went up the ladder but saw no sign of the girl. Doc and Sanchez were smiling when he came down. Raider gritted his teeth. "Let's get the hell out of here."

Sanchez turned toward Doc. "I think your partner cares a bit too much for the ladies."

"Most assuredly," Doc replied.

Raider pointed a finger at both of them. "Just find us a place to sleep where we won't get our throats cut."

That wiped the grins from their faces.

They chose a ledge on the boundary of the lower forests, a place high enough on the mountain to keep watch on the trail and the valley below.

Raider volunteered for the first watch, but Sanchez said they should all sleep. If the Totonacs or the Tiaxcalans decided to kill them, they would never see it coming. So Raider decided to sleep. The insects were not as plentiful in the cool mountain breeze, and he quickly dropped off. He opened an eye when he felt the warmth next to him.

Somehow he knew immediately that it was the girl. He smelled her. Then her hair fell into his face. She did not speak, which was all right with him since he didn't want to wake the others.

Her hands found the knotty bumps of his chest and stomach. She wanted to work him up. He knew why. They were going to throw her into the mountain because she was pure. She didn't want to be pure anymore.

Raider had never taken to busting cherries, but he figured he would be doing her a favor, what with her life on the line. He pulled her down beside him and started to kiss her. She was inexperienced, but she managed to catch on after a few minutes.

Raider's fingers slipped up her legs, into the flimsy cloth of her sacrificial gown. When her thighs parted, he felt the moistness below her pubic mound. Her own hands had strayed to his crotch, groping for the lump that protruded from the leg of his cutoff pants.

The girl gave a slight whimper when she felt the massive length in her hand. She drew back for a moment. Raider put a finger to her lips.

"Shh. You want to go swimmin' in that mountain back yonder?"

He pulled down his cutoffs and guided her hand back to his prick. The girl began to breathe heavily as she stroked him. Raider nuzzled her breasts, licking the tight nipples. He slipped a finger into her, only to have her moan again.

The big man rolled over, settling in between her thighs. "Just gonna have to get this over with."

Sweat broke out on his body as he bumped his prickhead against the soft folds of her female prize. He had never knowingly popped a virgin before. But if he didn't, she would just go to one of the others. And it was his damned reward for saving her from that spook doctor.

Her eyes peered up at him, begging for release from her purity. He lowered his hips, sinking several inches inside her. The girl cried out, almost shouting her pleasure/pain into the night. Raider cupped a hand over her mouth, but it was too late.

Doc stirred and sat up. "Raider? What is it?"

"Nothin'." Then: "The girl came back."

"Oh. Ohhh, I see. And I trust she's no longer fit for volcano duty."

"Shut up and go back to sleep, Doc."

Sanchez sat up as well. "Señors, are we being attacked?"

"No," Doc replied. "The girl is back, and Raider is making sure that she has no purity left to sacrifice."

His cock was half in and half out of her. "Both of you shut up and go back to sleep." She was smiling up at him, her face contorted in pleasant agony.

When the others had settled in again, Raider continued his motion, gradually increasing the depth of his explorations. She turned out to be a pretty big girl after all, able to take his entire length on her first try. And she seemed to be getting the hang of it.

Her hips began to move on their own, picking up Raider's slow rhythm. The pace increased as the big man stopped thinking of her as a former virgin. She was only a woman, tight around him with each slippery penetration. Raider's body bucked as he approached climax. He waited until the last moment before he withdrew and deposited his discharge on her stomach.

She looked up with confusion in her eyes.

"No *muchacha*. No baby," he said.

She did not seem to understand. He kissed her cheek and she smiled again. Above them, the mountain rumbled, but she was no longer fodder for the gods. The tribe would have to find another virgin to feed to the mountain.

Raider slipped his arm around her and pulled her closer to him. She melted into his body, rubbing her face in his chest. Raider peered up at the sky full of stars. It didn't look much like the Texas sky, but then again they were a long damn way from home.

He looked back down at the girl. "Maybe we can take you home tomorrow, little darlin'. Course, I don't guess your tribe will want to see you, unless we can cook up some story that they'll believe."

"Raider," Doc called. "I don't mind your licentious behavior, but your talking is keeping me awake."

"Hell, Doc, I was just thinkin' this girl could help to get us into the Indian village down yonder."

"Hmm, worth a thought," Doc replied. "But in the morning."

"Yep. Whatever you say."

Raider closed his eyes. He was drifting off when the girl renewed her interest in the flaccid member between his legs. Apparently she had enjoyed the initial round so much that she was coming back for seconds. Raider rolled over and obliged her.

When they were finished, he dozed off with the girl wrapped in his arms. He half expected her to be gone the next morning, but she was still sleeping beside him when the sun peaked over the mountain. He might have revived her for a final tumble, but he found himself possessed of another natural burden.

So he rose, as he had for nearly every morning of his life, in search of relief. The girl would be waiting for him, warm and eager. If he could just return to her before the others woke up.

He urinated and then turned back toward their encampment. His black eyes grew wide. He reached for the Colt but he knew it wouldn't help much. There were too many Indians descending from a higher slope, and they were swarming all over Doc and the others.

CHAPTER ELEVEN

Raider had to try something. He raised the Colt and fired a slug into the chest of a Totonac warrior who had been hovering over the girl. As soon as he fell, another painted Indian appeared to take his place. Raider only had two more slugs. He thumbed back the hammer, trying to remember the last time he had killed a man with his bare hands. But he never got off the second burst.

A Totonac jumped him from behind. Raider shifted his weight and tossed the runty Indian over his shoulder. When the man landed in front of him, Raider swung the butt of the Colt into his brightly painted jaw, causing the man to buckle and fall to the ground.

Raider wheeled back to his right, searching for the other members of his party. "Doc!"

Four men were holding the man from Boston. A hoard of warriors had surrounded Tommy and Sanchez. Raider could not risk a shot, not with his compatriots in the line of fire. So he charged like a mad bull with one spike in his hump, oblivious to the matador's blade.

Doc cried out for him to give it up, but there wasn't much quit inside the big man. A warrior in front of Doc dropped to one knee, lifted a flimsy bow, and notched a short-shafted arrow. Raider didn't see him, or he would never have run squarely into the path of the arrow. The point lodged in the meat of his shoulder.

Raider stopped in his tracks. He looked down at the shard of wood that protruded from his body. The arrow hadn't gone in too deep. It really didn't hurt that bad. He reached for the blood-flecked shaft, but he couldn't seem to get a grip on it.

His head had started to spin. Something on the arrow tip. He looked up at Doc, who was saying something he could not hear.

Raider's lips barely moved. "Poison." Then he fell to the ground and lost consciousness.

Eight arms restrained Doc as he tried to reach his partner. Sanchez grabbed his shoulder as well. "Señor, there is nothing you can do."

"Is he dead?"

Sanchez lowered his head. "I do not know. Sometimes the poison kills, sometimes it doesn't."

One of the painted warriors barked an order. Four men lifted Raider's body from the ground. Doc wondered if he imagined the slow rise and fall of his partner's chest.

"Damn them."

"It is not their fault, señor."

Doc glared at Sanchez. "What do you mean?"

"They did not want to kill us. Raider should not have fought."

Before Doc could reply, a spear point urged him forward. They started downward on a narrow trail that wound into a peaceful stretch of forest. When they slipped into a clearing, Doc raised his eyes to the huge structure before him. The Pyramid of the Sun. And the old man with the golden robes stood ready for them, his arms outstretched like a father welcoming home a prodigal son.

The old man's hair was completely white. He smiled weakly when he saw Doc. His voice came out of his chest like the sour chord of a broken squeeze-box. He was beyond sixty years of age, perhaps more. The man from Boston was puzzled by the first words from the old man's mouth.

"White men," he said dotingly. "I haven't see a white man in ten years. Come forward."

He urged Doc to take his place at the base of the pyramid's steps. Doc gazed up into the old man's white face. He had not been exposed to the sun, not like the Indians who seemed to worship him.

Doc struck a proud pose. "Sir, I demand to know your name and why you have brought us here."

The old man nodded. "They call me, Bringer of Gold."

Sanchez raised a finger at their unlikely host. "Did you steal the gold? From Santa Anna. Did you take it fifty years ago?"

"Yes," Doc chimed in. "Did you purloin the booty that was meant for Colonel Sam Houston?"

The old man seemed stunned for a moment, but then he smiled and raised his hands to heaven. "Praise the true Christian God. It took fifty years, but He sent somebody to find me."

Doc suddenly felt weak in the knees. "Tell me, sir, do I have the pleasure of addressing Jim Bowie or Davy Crockett?"

The man's clotted eyes dropped to meet Doc's gaze. "Come, sir. If you will accompany me to the . . ." His eyes fell on the girl. "What's this? I thought she was—"

"My partner saved her," Doc said. "He was felled by one of your arrows."

The old man rubbed his chin. "This isn't good. If the Tiaxcalans find out . . ."

"But how can they?" Sanchez offered.

"Word travels faster than you could possibly imagine, my friend." The old man sighed. "Ah, but it does not matter now. Take her back to the volcano and—"

Doc forced his hand. "She is no longer pure."

The old man's eyes narrowed. "Your partner?"

Doc nodded. He wondered where they had taken Raider's body. Would he ever see the big man from Arkansas again? His mind drifted back to the matters at hand. The old man gestured for them to accompany him up the stairs of the pyramid. Doc and Sanchez followed, with Tommy in their footsteps. They took one stair at a time, easily keeping pace with the old man's feeble gait.

About halfway up the ancient structure, the old man stopped and pressed a rock in the green wall. A wall of stone slid back, revealing an ornate inner chamber. The old man held out his hand. "After you, gentlemen."

Doc, Sanchez, and Tommy slipped through the archway, into a shadowy room full of gold. Bizarre-looking figurines of soft yellow stared at them with bulging golden eyes. Idols formed a semicircle around a golden throne. In front of the throne was an open chest of gold.

"Incredible!" Sanchez said.

The old man stepped up behind them, touching another stone that closed the wall. "I brought their gold back to them. When I left Texas, I ran as far as I could. Fate brought me here. When they saw my gold, they dropped to their knees. The foolish savages. They never even explored this temple. I found this room my second day here. There's another chamber further up. That's where I reside."

Doc challenged the old man with his eyes. "The reigning god of gold?"

Smiling, the high priest of the pyramid ascended his throne. "I am the master of all I survey. How many men can say that?"

Doc's brow wrinkled. "But you stole money that was intended for the forces of Sam Houston. You took it from the Alamo, deserting your fellows."

"I was never at the Alamo!" the old man cried. "My partner and I found that money ourselves. We ambushed a squad of Santa Anna's men."

Sanchez bristled. "So you figured the money was yours to keep?"

He nodded. "There was no way we could get it back through enemy lines. So we ran south, away from the Mexicans."

"Sir, I believe it is time for you to tell us exactly who you are." Doc had said it matter-of-factly. "Spare none of the details. Several men have died already, my partner among them."

The old man leaned back as if he were exhausted. "I am Eustus Frazier, gentlemen. Formerly of the Texas militia. Although I haven't seen the territory of Texas for nearly fifty years."

"It's a state now," Doc replied. "Frazier? Wait a minute, there was a letter in Morton's strongbox addressed to a man named Frazier. It was also signed by a man named Morton."

Eustus Frazier sat up straight. "I never saw such a letter."

"Forgery," Doc said. "Hmm . . . so, would you mind telling us who your partner was in this escapade? Perhaps Jim Bowie or Davy Crockett?"

Frazier glared at Doc. "How could you think two such fine men would be involved in something like I did?"

"Then who helped you?" Sanchez asked.

Frazier shook his tired head. "I promised him I would never tell if someone came for the gold. When my partner went back to Texas, he took his share."

Doc asked if the partner went back to San Antonio. The old man didn't know. He didn't even know if his partner had made it back alive.

Doc decided to go in another direction. "Mr. Frazier, I would like to remind you that a man was killed in San Antonio, a man named Hollis Morton. You see, one of his relatives, a man with the same initials as yourself, E.F., was trying to blackmail him into financing an expedition to recover the Mexican gold. Our involvement in this case led us down here to you. Only, the blackmailer suggested that Davy Crockett and Jim Bowie were involved in your caper."

"I deny that," Frazier said emphatically.

"Then who?" Doc urged. "You must tell us."

Frazier shook his head again. "I promised."

"Was it Hollis Morton?" Doc asked.

"No."

Sanchez scoffed. "Can't you see he has forgotten? He is so old."

"A nice try," Frazier replied. "But you're wrong. I can see his face as clearly as if it were yesterday."

"That knowledge might lead us to the killer back in San Antonio. We must know the identity of your partner."

The mountain rumbled outside. Frazier looked back over his shoulder. "Don't worry, gents, she hasn't blown yet. We'll have to scare up another girl."

"You heathen," Sanchez cried. "Have you taken the ways of these savages to heart?"

"A man can get used to anything," Frazier replied.

"But why," Doc said. "Why did you flee like a coward? For this?"

"I was young then." Frazier gestured around him. "And I am the king here. I was nobody in Texas."

Another trembling from the volcano.

Doc felt weak in his legs. "Mr. Frazier, as agents of both governments, Mexican and American, I must advise you to consider yourself under arrest. We are going to take you back along with the gold."

Frazier smiled a brown-toothed grin. "I don't think my subjects would like that, sir."

Sanchez pointed his finger. "They will let you go if you give the order. Tell them that you are going back for more gold."

"The treasure must be returned to the Mexican government," Doc rejoined. "And you must go back to clear the names of Davy Crockett and Jim Bowie."

"I did not blacken their names," Frazier insisted. "And the treasure is not going back to the Mexicans."

"Don't make us use force," Doc said.

Frazier gestured toward the sliding wall. "Go out and argue with my minions, sir."

Sanchez looked at Doc. "He's right. We are outnumbered."

"Not if we take him as a hostage," Doc replied. "They wouldn't harm us if we had a knife to his throat." Doc slung his pack off his shoulder. "I still have my Diamondback here somewhere."

"No, you don't."

The voice had come from the other side of the room. Doc and Sanchez wheeled toward Tommy, who had been hiding in the shadows. The lad was suddenly possessed of a voice. And he was holding Doc's Diamondback on them. The short barrel was aimed at Eustus Frazier, the old man on the throne.

CHAPTER TWELVE

Tommy was no longer a deaf-mute. He waved the pistol at Frazier, smiling. "Hello, Uncle Eustus."

Doc stared down the barrel of his own weapon. "You! But how?"

"We're determined in the Frazier family. Allow me. I am Ezra Morton Frazier. Hollis Morton was my great-uncle. Your half brother, Uncle Eustus."

"Then Morton was your partner!" Doc accused.

"No," Frazier insisted. "I didn't even know I had a half brother."

Ezra Frazier smiled. "He didn't know it either until I informed him."

Doc wore a puzzled look that reflected the sudden blossoming of his professional sensibilities. "But how? How were you able to piece everything together? The gold, the trek to Mexico?"

Ezra gestured toward his uncle with the gun barrel. "My uncle is a vain man. He could not resist writing a letter home. He sent it from Tampico. He said he was going deep into the jungle with his gold. I don't think he ever thought it would reach my great-aunt, the woman he left behind. But she had it in her attic. She showed it to me right before she died. Her last request was that I find you, Uncle Eustus."

Sanchez glared at the young man. "How did you fall in

with Doc and Raider? How could you have known about their plan?"

Ezra smiled. "Can't you guess?"

"Of course," Doc cried. "Someone on the inside."

"My uncle's *real* partner. He knew about it. He was the one who helped me to blackmail Morton."

"Was it his idea to murder Morton?" Doc asked.

"No," Ezra replied. "I came up with that on my own. In fact, he was against my forcing my hand. But you see, I had to do something. Life in the circus wasn't very lucrative. You know how much an acrobat is paid? Less than a cowboy."

"So you knew of the sloop before we did," Doc said.

Ezra smiled. "That was a work of genius. I had to hurry like hell to get to Galveston. Then I had to kill the captain's first mate. He took me on at the last minute. I played the deaf-mute so you would talk freely around me."

Sanchez scowled at the former mute. "Two murders. How many more?"

"As many as it takes," replied the nephew of the Bringer of Gold. "But now we should make plans for taking this gold back to civilization."

Sanchez and Doc refused to move. "We're not helping you," Doc insisted.

"No," Sanchez rejoined. "You have taken charge here. As your uncle said, go out and face his—"

The temple began to shake. Another tremor through the earth. When the rumbling started, Sanchez sprang toward the young man. The Diamondback went off. Sanchez fell with blood pouring from his chest.

Doc started for the fallen colonel, but he lost his balance and fell to the floor. He heard something click behind him. The old man lifted a worn, rusty flintlock pistol. Fire flashed from the muzzle-loading weapon.

Ezra Frazier clutched his bicep where the lead ball had grazed him. He grimaced and then fired a return volley at his uncle. The slug caught the old man in the forehead. He fell from his throne next to Doc.

When the trembling subsided, Doc regained his feet. He looked at the dead bodies and then glared at the young man he had once trusted. "Are you happy now, Tommy? Oh, excuse me, I mean Ezra."

The young man motioned with the barrel of the Diamondback. "You're gonna help me take this gold out of here, Pinkerton." He pressed the rock that opened the stone wall. "We'll just take the chest. The other things stay."

"You'll never get this through the jungle."

Ezra nodded. "You're right. That's why I'm bringing you along. We can follow the path we cut the first time."

The mountain rumbled again. Doc laughed. "You don't plan to take this chest over that volcano."

"I'll make these stupid Indians help us."

"I'm sure they'll jump to it when they discover that you killed their high priest."

He waved the gun at Doc. "Just shut up! Grab that chest and pull it outside. Now!"

The chest of coins was small but so heavy that Doc had to pull it an inch at a time. He moved slowly, hoping . . . what could he hope? That the Totonac would discover their dead leader? Who would they blame? The white men, of course.

"Hurry, Pinkerton."

When the chest was clear of the temple, Frazier pressed the rock to close the wall. The sliding stone made a noise that resembled the roar from the smoking mountain. When it was shut, Doc realized the noise was still coming from the volcano. He looked down the steps of the pyramid to see the Totonacs gathering at the base of their shrine.

"They're looking for someone to save them," Doc offered. "You want to go down there and tell them that their only hope is lying on the floor with a slug in his head?"

"Shut up"

The volcano spoke to them again.

Doc tried to smile. "You know, Ezra, the Aztecs believed that the world would end for them one day."

"I said to shut up!"

"When Cortez arrived, I suppose it did."

Ezra swung the pistol at Doc. The man from Boston ducked the blow and came up with a hard right to the lad's breadbasket. Frazier buckled to the ground. Doc stamped on his wrist and removed the gun from his hand.

"Now you are my prisoner, Mr. Frazier. You will return to San Antonio to stand trial for the murder of Hollis Morton." The mountain reminded Doc that they were in trouble. "Providing, of course, that we get out alive. Now it is your turn to drag the chest. Shall we go? I'm waiting, Mr. Frazier. Several men have died for this gold. Would you like to be among their number?"

Doc felt just angry enough to shoot him right then. Frazier must have seen the look in his eye. He stood up and fixed his hands on the handles of the chest. Doc turned back toward the Indians below, wondering how he would convince them to let him leave. He never got to ask.

Howling shrieks resounded from the trees. Doc and Frazier both gazed up to see the rival tribe advancing from the forest. The Tiaxcalans had obviously received news of the unsuccessful sacrifice. Now they were riding down on the Totonacs to make them pay for angering the volcano demon.

Arrows and spears flew through the air, wedging in the flesh of the Totonacs. Some of the warriors ran out to meet the invasion, but there weren't enough of them.

Doc wheeled toward Frazier. "I'm afraid we must part company, my friend."

Frazier was staring at the onrushing horde. "You can't just leave me. They'll kill me."

"Pardon me if I don't shed any tears."

Doc started down the steps of the pyramid.

"You can't leave me!"

Doc didn't hear him. Frazier had his gold. Good luck getting it back to a place where he could spend it. As far as Doc was concerned, the only thing on his mind was saving his own life. Frazier kept crying out behind him, but the man from Boston had no intention of stopping. He ran forward with his Diamondback in hand, wondering how much longer he would be possessed of his life.

The first wave of Tiaxcalans had been delayed by the stronger warriors in the Totonac tribe. Doc reached the base of the pyramid in time to see the Tiaxcalans breaking through the front line. The remainder of the Totonac tribe fled in all directions, some making for the trees, others running straight toward the mountain. Doc spied several feather-clad Indians heading due north. They seemed to be the priests, like the one Raider had killed. Perhaps they knew where they were going. He started after them.

Suddenly the priests were set upon by a multitude of Tiaxcalan warriors. Arrows pierced their hearts. Doc fired, killing one of the warriors and attracting the attention of the others. They started after him. Doc broke into a full run, heading back toward the temple.

Shafts of wood whizzed by his head. As he neared the base of the pyramid, his foot caught on a rock in the ground. Doc tumbled down, landing hard on his chest. The air was forced from his lungs. He lay there gasping for breath. The Tiaxcalans surrounded him, their cold eyes peering down from painted faces. One of them muttered something and pointed at the mountain. He was blaming the intruders for displeasing the gods.

The sentence was death. He raised a spear, intending to impale Doc's chest. The man from Boston closed his eyes, awaiting his climb to glory. Instead he heard a tune that in no way resembled a harp. It was the familiar music of a Winchester rifle.

The spearman buckled and fell forward. The others turned toward the temple to see the smoke from the rifle barrel. Raider cranked in another round and dispatched a second warrior to his demise. When the second man fell, the rest of the Tiaxcalans ran away from Doc. Raider chased them on with repeated bursts from the Winchester.

Doc staggered to his feet. Raider came down the steps to greet him. The big man's skin had a green pallor to it.

Doc looked at the shining new rifle. "Where'd you get that?"

Raider patted the stock of the Winchester. "I woke up in a room full of weapons. Somebody had wrapped this in leather. It's a' old one, but it seems to work all right."

Doc nodded. "Frazier was probably well equipped. I imagine he traded some of his gold for them."

A war cry resounded from the temple. Raider wheeled to see an Indian aiming a bow at them. Raider popped him quickly with a hip-burst from the rifle. The Indian fell from the pyramid, cascading down the sloping wall.

The big man looked wide-eyed at his partner. "What the hell did I wake up to, Doc? Where the hell is Sanchez? And Tommy?"

Before Doc could utter a word they were faced by two more Tiaxcalan warriors. Raider had to shoot fast to get them both. He reached back into his pockets, which were stuffed with cartridges from the old man's arsenal.

"Hey, Doc, how about fillin' in what happened while I was asleep?"

Doc regarded his partner's sickly-looking face. "You were obviously under the spell of some sort of narcotic. I'm surprised you weren't killed."

"Yeah, so how's about—"

A crashing noise behind them, from the steps of the temple. Raider aimed the gun at the young man who hovered over the gold. The chest had fallen down the incline to shatter at the pyramid's base.

"Tommy!"

"No," Doc replied. "His name is Ezra Frazier. He killed Morton and wormed his way into our expedition."

Raider's eyes narrowed. "You're shittin' me?"

"Would that I were."

"Where's Sanchez?"

Doc pointed at Ezra Frazier. "Dead. Killed by him."

Raider aimed the Winchester. "I'm gonna take him out, Doc."

But the ground began to shake again. Doc and Raider both lost their balance. An explosion resounded from the hole in the smoking mountain. A second eruption followed. Ash and soot began to rain down on them. Cries from both tribes of Indians pierced the dirty air. Revenge was quickly forgotten. Suddenly they were all running for their lives, including the two Pinkertons who were a long way from home.

CHAPTER THIRTEEN

When the mountain exploded, Ezra Frazier tried to gather up as much gold as he could carry. He ran headlong for the path that would take him back to the jungle. The volcano would not stop him, he thought. Nothing would stop him. His plan had been too elaborate to be thwarted by one of nature's forces. As he neared the rim of the crater, he knew he was right.

The mountain was no longer smoking. A sulphurous smell permeated the air. Frazier looked back at the cloud of ash that rained down on the Pyramid of the Sun. Frazier laughed. The fool Indians were scurrying about like frightened ants, while he was safe above them.

He flipped his head upward, searching for the rope ladder that led to the rim of the crater. Once he was on the other side, he would have no trouble retracing the path through the jungle. Sanchez had shown him how to live in there. Once he reached the river, he could construct a raft and float downstream. No one would suspect a deaf-mute of such glorious escapades. He could wait for a boat to take him from Tampico. He would be home free when he returned to Texas.

As his hand reached for the bottom rung of the ladder, Frazier heard a bubbling above him. Something hissed, like a rattler—or like water when something hot hits the surface. He suddenly felt the heat emanating from above.

When he looked up, he screamed. A red, molten substance was leaking over the rim of the crater, coming slowly as it oozed from the hole in the smoking mountain. The lava engulfed Ezra Frazier and his gold, pushing the little man back toward the pyramid, burying him forever in a sheet of liquid rock, sealing his body alongside the treasure.

"Holy God, Doc! What the hell is that?"

Raider was staring up at the sudden flow of red.

"Lava," Doc replied. "We should be thankful it's not coming a great deal faster."

They had been heading north, the same direction taken by the priests Doc had seen earlier. When the lava began to flow, they decided to run. If they could reach high ground, the red-hot river might not catch up to them. The narrow path carried them to a stream where three dugout canoes waited on the bank.

Doc shook his head, smiling. "Leave it to a holy man to plan his exit. For all their invocation of the gods, they're the first ones to abandon their deities."

"With the congregation runnin', why should the preacher play the fool?" Raider offered.

Doc jumped into one of the dugouts. "I don't mean to be rude, but we haven't much time."

"Be rude, Doc. Be as rude as you want."

Raider leapt in behind his partner. They started down the stream, which widened quickly. Raider dug the pole into the streambed when he saw the line of canoes ahead of them.

"Tiaxcalans," Doc said.

"What?"

Doc raised his Diamondback. "Hostile Indians."

"Hell, we didn't do nothin' to them."

"It doesn't matter," Doc replied. "They aren't going to let us pass."

Raider took aim with the rifle. "Let's see how they like this."

He fired, but they quickly ducked under his slugs. Doc was right anyway—it didn't matter, they could never kill all of them. Raider grabbed the pole and directed the canoe into the brush When they were hidden, he glared at his partner.

"Any ideas, Doc?"

The Tiaxcalans were getting closer. Doc reached for his pack. He withdrew the three sticks of sweaty dynamite. As he lashed them together, he could hear the breaking of trees in the forest. The lava pushed forward, igniting everything in its path.

Doc looked back at Raider. "Get ready with that rifle."

Raider levered a cartridge into the chamber of the decade-old weapon. "You tell me what to do."

"Get out of the boat."

"What?"

Doc gestured toward the bank. "Get out and stand on the shore. Find a spot where you can see the canoe and the Indians as they approach."

"But I don't—"

"Just do it," Doc said in a rasping whisper. "You'll understand when you see what I have in mind."

With that, the big man from Arkansas slid onto the shore. He took a few steps forward, pushing away the brush. The Tiaxcalans were almost on them. He looked back, but Doc was gone.

"Weatherbee, you son of bitch!"

He cast his eyes on the water again. Their canoe floated downstream toward the Tiaxcalan vessels. But Doc was no longer sitting in the small craft. Where the hell was he?

The Indians halted when they saw the canoe floating toward them. Raider scanned the bow of the dugout, wondering if Doc was laying low. It was then that he saw the three sticks of dynamite wedged into the bow. There wasn't any blasting cap on them, but that didn't matter. With the shafts sweating nitro, the rifle would be enough.

Raider took careful aim. "Steady." The boat neared the Tiaxcalans. One of the warriors reached toward the bow. Raider fired off a burst, chipping the wood next to the charge.

"Son of a bitch." He levered the rifle and fired again. The second slug found its target. The water kicked up, destroying the canoes in the circle of the explosion. Raider fell to the ground under the force of the dynamite. His chest felt tight, but he was able to suck air in a few moments.

"Raider, damn you, don't just stand there. Come on!"

Doc held a canoe steady in the current of the stream. He had swum back to the other dugouts. Raider quickly waded out to the vessel and rolled over the side into the canoe. He snapped up when he heard the crackling forest behind them. The lava moved steadily through the foliage, incinerating the leaves and branches.

"Can we outrun it, Doc?"

"I suppose we shall see."

They poled like madmen, slipping through the carnage from the dynamite. The water hissed behind them as the lava flowed into the stream. Raider looked back, expecting to be engulfed by the molten rock. He spun back around when Doc cried out.

Suddenly the lava didn't seem as important as the waterfall ahead. The stream frothed over a bed of rocks just before it tumbled downward. There was no way to tell how far the falls dropped. It really didn't matter. They couldn't stay behind to face the volcano's red-hot offering.

Raider held tightly to the Winchester. "Let's get out of the boat, Doc. We got a better chance."

Doc went over the side, struggling in the current. Raider joined him, trying to keep the rifle over his head. The canoe swung in the rapids, twirling clockwise toward the falls.

As they were swept on by the current, Raider was suddenly thinking about a little white church near the farm where he had grown up in Arkansas. He remembered the sound of the choir, the smell of Sunday best, the anticipation of fried chicken for dinner. He felt the draw of gravity as he tumbled over behind the canoe. For a moment he was suspended in an effortless fall. He felt a sense of elation, a carefree sensation that had to precede death. He let go of the rifle when he hit a deep pool at the bottom. His legs didn't break. He struggled toward the surface, gasping for air.

When his head broke free, he smelled the sulphur from the volcano. He treaded water for a moment, turning in a circle to look for Doc. He saw his partner's sandy head bobbing in the pool. Doc had grabbed the side of the dugout, which seemed to have survived the fall.

"Hey, Weatherbee, are we dead?"

Doc swung into the dugout. "Not yet." He used his hands

to paddle over to Raider. The big man joined his partner in the boat.

Doc gazed back toward the smoking mountain. "I don't know if we have a chance. I suppose if we follow the stream . . ."

Raider was peering down into the pool. "Do I have enough time to dive up that rifle?"

Something floated by the canoe. It was an arm. A piece of a dead Tiaxcalan. Doc's dynamite had shattered them.

"We'd better go now," said the man from Boston. "We can run downstream for a while. There." He pointed toward a pole that floated in the pool.

Raider picked up the pole and pushed them toward the stream that flowed out of the pool. He didn't even look back at the smoking mountain. And it wasn't until late the next day, when they had left the valley, that he even bothered to ask Doc about the complications that had transpired while he was asleep.

The canoe was resting on a sandy stretch of riverbank. Doc reclined on the sand with a banana in his hand. He didn't know the name of the river, only that it flowed east. He fully expected the water to end soon, forcing them to travel by foot.

Raider stood on the sandbar, peering back toward the western mountains. They could no longer see Totonac country. Even the mountain's rumbling had become inaudible. Doc had said that it wasn't a bad eruption, but Raider couldn't figure out what a *good* one would be.

The big man grabbed a banana from the stalk and sat down next to his partner. "Now let me see if I got this straight. Tommy was the one who planted them letters on Morton?"

Doc nodded. "Yes, he was trying to convince Morton that he should finance an expedition to Mexico. In reality, however, Morton knew nothing of Frazier or his dirty dealings."

Raider shook his head. "What about the Mexican gold piece?"

Doc shrugged. "He could have gotten it at a coin dealer or somewhere in Mexico. He was clever. That old letter looked real enough."

"Sure as hell. But how did he find out about the ship we was comin' on?"

"Think about it," Doc offered.

Raider's head snapped up. "An inside man?"

"Tommy—that is, Frazier—practically admitted it."

Raider scratched his matted skull. "Okay, but what about that coonskin cap at the condor cheater's place?"

"That could have been an offering to the old man. Those types of caps were worn more freely back then. Or Frazier's partner could have planted it as part of the ruse. I suppose we had better return to San Antonio and ask the man who went with Mr. Frazier."

Raider looked sideways at his partner. "You got any ideas about who that might be?"

Doc stood up and looked around him. "I think we had better get back to civilization first. Then we can ask the appropriate questions."

Raider nodded. He knew exactly what his partner was talking about. They weren't out of the woods yet. And all they really knew about the terrain was that the stream ran due east, around the mountains. They slipped back into the boat and poled out into the current, riding the water as far as it would take them.

CHAPTER FOURTEEN

The stream carried them as far as the lowlands due south of San Luis Potosí. From there, they walked for two days before coming on a group of farmers. Raider knew enough Spanish to ascertain that they were another three days from San Luis Potosí, where they would find the first tattered edges of civilization. The farmers did not know if there was a wire at the small ouptost.

Doc and Raider thanked the farmers and walked on. The going was tough in the heat, but there were plenty of waterholes along the way. The farmers had given them a skin and some tortillas. Fruit was not as plentiful here in the lowlands. Raider managed to rig up a slingshot that brought down an animal that vaguely resembled a raccoon.

They were mostly quiet, keeping a steady pace as they pushed northward. Raider could see Doc's mind working. The man from Boston assembled pieces of the puzzle in his head. He would know where to point the finger when they got back to San Antonio. *If* they ever got back to San Antonio.

Raider stopped suddenly and threw out his arm.

Doc came to a halt and looked up.

Four men on horseback stood in their path. The men were wearing brownish uniforms. All of them held rifles.

"Federales," Raider said. "And I don't have a gun."

Doc peered toward the soldiers. "But they are representatives of the law, after all. I mean, they are agents of the militia."

"Tell them that," the big man replied.

"But—"

"You don't seem to get my drift, Doc. They're the law out here. They can do whatever they want to us, and we can't do nothin' but holler."

"And you're certain they're evil?"

Raider shrugged. "Can't tell that till we talk to them. Even if they are rotten, it won't do us no good to run."

The *federales* wore sly grins as Doc and Raider approached them. Raider started to say something in Spanish, but a fat man, the sergeant, told them that he spoke English. The sergeant laughed when Raider said they had come from Zacatecas.

"Nobody comes out of Zacatecas alive, señor. You don't really expect me to believe that, do you?"

Doc stiffened like an indignant gentleman. "Sir, if you will take me to your superior, I will clear up this matter at once."

The sergeant swung down off his horse, leveling his rifle at them. "I don't think you want to see my commander, señor. He will only do to you what I must do."

Raider scowled at the sergeant. "And what's that?"

When he smiled, Doc saw that the sergeant was missing a tooth. "Señor, you are two gringos in a place where you should not be. I can take you to jail, or I can shoot you."

"See here," Doc cried. "We are agents of Allan Pinkerton, working with the Mexican government to recover a fortune in treasure."

The sergeant laughed. "I don't see no treasure."

"Of course you don't," Doc replied. "It was lost when the volcano exploded and the temple was covered with lava."

"Temple, señor? I don't see no temple. And I don't know what a volcano is. It is a mystery to me."

Doc gestured with his hands. "A smoking mountain. Debris, lava. Please, I entreat you, take us to your commanding officer or the regional governor. You will see that I am telling the truth."

One of the sergeant's men muttered something in Spanish.

Raider exhaled and looked at his partner. "That one says he wants to shoot us."

The sergeant grinned. "We must do something to you. Unless you have something to give us. Do you have something to give us, so we won't kill you, señor gringo?"

Doc threw up his hands. "I am at a loss, sir."

Raider spat on the ground. "To hell with you, sergeant. My partner and me ain't takin' no guff off a bunch of wetbacks. Go ahead and shoot us."

The sergeant did not take kindly to Raider's slur. He ordered one of his men to tie their hands behind their backs. Raider would not let the man near him.

"I ain't lettin' you hog-tie me. Just shoot me and git it over with."

The sergeant ordered his men to line up in a firing squad. When they were ready, he turned back to Doc and Raider. "I don't have to do this, señor. If you will take back what you called me, I won't—"

"Do your worst, beaner!" Raider cried.

The sergeant raised his hand. "Ready."

"This is ridiculous," Doc said.

"Aim."

Raider pointed a finger. "If Colonel Sanchez was here, he would—"

"F . . . anh?" The sergeant glared at the big man.

"I said, if Colonel Sanchez was here, he'd blister your butt good!"

The sergeant ordered his men to lower their rifles. "Where is Colonel Sanchez? Tell me, gringo!"

"He died back there in the jungle," Raider replied. "He was with us most of the way."

"Yes," Doc rejoined. "He died valiantly trying to save my life. A finer man I have never met."

The sergeant crossed himself. "I served under Colonel Sanchez. We were dispatched here to wait for his return, to look for him."

Raider threw up his hands. "That's what I've been tryin' to tell you. We was right with him all the way."

Doc raised his hand. "If you take us to your commanding officer, we will report at once to your government."

When the sergeant clapped his hands, his men returned to their mounts.

Raider breathed easier. "That's more like it."

The sergeant put a finger in the big man's chest. "Just one thing, señor. You must take back the names you called me."

"Sure, sarge. I'm sorry I called you a wetback and a beaner. Are you sorry you called me a gringo?"

For a moment, Doc was worried that the sergeant might take offense. But the fat man only laughed and swung his mount north. Doc and Raider had to walk behind them for a long time before they saw the rooftops of San Luis Potosí.

The soldiers threw them into a dank, dark cell that smelled like horse manure. They brought beans and tortillas that were hot. The sergeant served them fresh, cold water in wooden cups. When Doc asked him how long they would have to wait, the sergeant simply replied that they should be patient.

Two days later, Raider was ready to try some sort of move. He figured they could jump the guard and overpower him. If they could get out of the cell, they might be able to steal a few weapons and shoot their way out. Of course, even if they broke free, they would still have the entire Mexican Army on their asses. It didn't look too good.

Doc voted down the escape plan, and he proved to be right. On the third day, the sergeant called for them and led them out of the cell. He saw to it that both Pinkertons enjoyed a hot bath and a change of clothes. When they were clean, the sergeant led them down a narrow street to a big hacienda in the middle of town. A man in uniform waited for them in the main parlor of the house.

"That will be all, Sergeant." His tone was imperial. The man regarded Doc and Raider. "The sergeant tells me that you two claim to be the men who went into the jungle with Colonel Sanchez."

Doc nodded. "We are agents for the Pinkerton National Detective Agency. We were assigned to work with the colonel to recover a certain cache of gold. We had an order signed by General Díaz himself—"

"I am General Díaz," the man replied.

Raider's jaw hung open. "What? I thought Díaz was the

head of this whole blamed country."

"And so I am," Díaz replied. "Would you gentlemen care for a drink or a cigar while you tell me your story?"

"Whiskey for me," Raider said.

Doc felt his mouth watering. "I haven't had a cigar since . . . I can't remember when."

The general only laughed and called for a servant to fetch their needs.

When they were relaxed, Doc laid out the entire scheme for him. Frazier's deceit, the colonel's trickery, the trip upstream, the jungle, the smoking mountain, the colonel's death, and their escape. General Díaz shook his head.

"So the gold was lost after all. Claimed by the gods that rule the southlands." He sighed. "I suppose there should be some sort of reward for both of you, but unfortunately you were not successful in your mission."

Doc shrugged. "A cigar and a glass of tequila are reward enough."

"I'll say," Raider guffawed. "Hell, I never thought I'd see the light of day when that mountain went off."

Díaz watched them both with something that resembled admiration. "Your story is too fantastic not to be believed. I must tell you that I deemed this business important enough to come up here myself. That gold could have been very useful to me."

Raider shook his head, laughing derisively.

Díaz turned his cold eyes on the big man. "Do you find something funny, señor?"

Raider sat up straight, wiping the grin from his face. He had felt a surge in the general's voice, the power of authority. "Er, no, sir, I was just thinkin' that gold never did me much good. I mean, it don't seem to sit well with a common sort of man."

"Ask Ezra Frazier," Doc rejoined.

Díaz did not smile. "You cannot understand what it is like to be head of a country, señor. That gold would have been helpful to my people."

"Yes, sir," Raider replied. "I didn't mean to question it for a minute. I just wish we coulda brought it back."

Díaz focused on Doc. "One thing, Señor Weatherbee."

"Yes?"

"If I find out that either one of you has lied to me, you won't be able to hide. Not even when you are across the Rio Grande."

Doc cleared his throat. "I assure you, sir, that every word we have told you is the truth. There was no way for us to get the gold out of there. And now it is buried under tons of rock."

"And your case is ended," Díaz said.

"Not quite," Doc replied. "I was wondering, is there a wire in town?"

"Wire?"

"A telegraph. I'd like to send a message north."

Díaz shook his head. "I am sorry, señor, we do not have a telegraph this far south. However, you will be able to ride with me on the train north. I will have my men escort you to the border."

"Feel free to have one of your men accompany us back to San Antonio," Doc offered.

"No," Díaz replied. "I will trust you. If you are lying, I will find out sooner or later."

Raider bristled a little. "We ain't lyin'."

The general met his gaze, staring Raider down before he turned to leave the room.

When he was gone, Doc looked at the cigar. "Raider, we've shared drinks and tobacco with the head of the Mexican government."

"So?"

"Aren't you the least bit impressed?"

Raider threw back the rest of his tequila. "Hell, Doc, I was thinkin' he oughta be damned impressed by meetin' us. 'Specially after what we been through. Hell, I bet ol' Díaz there ain't seen as much action as us."

"I cannot believe your arrogance!"

"Doc, let's just get the hell out of Mexico."

For once the man from Boston thought his partner had a good idea.

CHAPTER FIFTEEN

They came north on the train, disembarking at the border of the United States. Raider stomped his big foot on the Texas earth, declaiming his joy at being home. Doc did not seem as impressed by their homecoming. The gentleman Pinkerton had been quiet their whole trip. Raider recognized the sly expression on Doc's countenance. He was ready to lower the boom on somebody. Raider figured he had to be ready as well.

"When we get to San Antone, I'm gonna need some cash, Doc. I know where I can get a good deal on a Peacemaker. This little guy who sells guns. He's from some foreign place, near Germany."

"Austria?" Doc offered.

Raider thought about it. "Maybe. Hell, I got to buy some boots, a Stetson. My holster's gone, I need a horse. You know somethin'? I missed Texas, if you can believe that. I actually missed Texas while I was down there." The big man peered at the dust that rose up in the distance. "Look there, Doc, the damned stage is right on time. We didn't even have to wait. By the way, Doc, I was thinkin' . . ."

Raider kept talking, but Doc did not follow what he was saying. Doc's mind had turned to the accoutrements of the city. Everything he had taken with him had been lost in Mexico.

He would have to outfit himself from top to bottom, including a new .38 Diamondback. "Make sure you bring your Colt with you, Raider. I'm going to nail him, and there's no telling what he might do."

"'Him', Doc?"

"You'll see. If I'm right, you'll see."

"Hell, Doc, you're always right."

The Concord coach screeched to a dusty halt. Doc and Raider entered the belly of the stage. They'd pay at the other end of the line, in San Antonio. The driver cracked his whip before the door was closed, heading northeast in a cloud of hoof dust.

Doc stood in Freemont Biddle's private study, telling his tale for Hardy Tabor and old Biddle himself. Raider figured it had to be one of them that Doc was going to finger. The big man voted for Tabor. He had a weasely look anyway. Hell, the old man looked like he was going to croak.

Doc told it well. Raider shuddered when he remembered. He had been dreaming about the damned volcano ever since they had gone over the waterfall. That stream had saved them!

When Doc had finished, Tabor leaned back and blew out a thankful breath. "So this Frazier was behind the entire thing. He made up the story about Crockett and Bowie to buffalo his uncle, Hollis Morton."

"Looks that way," Raider said. "Course, you might just know a little more than you're lettin' on, Hardy."

The governor's assistant cocked his head. "I don't know what you're talking about."

"Don't you?"

"Mr. Raider, if you have something to say..."

Doc interceded. "Gentlemen, please."

Biddle was wiping his forehead. "We don't want to hear any more from you, Weatherbee. It's a shame that the Mexicans are out some gold, but at least we have our good names back."

"An interesting choice of words," Doc replied.

Tabor slacked forward in his chair. "Will either of you make clear to me what you're trying to say?"

Doc took the lead. "My partner is right when he suggests that there's something more at stake here. You see, Eustus

Frazier had a partner. And that partner returned to the States, leaving Frazier behind."

Tabor shrugged. "So? Was his partner Davy Crockett or Jim Bowie?"

"No," Doc replied.

"Then we have nothing to worry about," Biddle said. He slammed his cane on the desk. "Thank you for your report, Mr. Weatherbee. I think you've told us enough."

Doc regarded the old gentleman's sweaty forehead. "It's quite cool in here, Mr. Biddle. And I have a bit more to tell you. I'm sure you'll want to hear my report before I take it to the Army and the state attorney."

Biddle slumped forward. "Let me hear it."

Tabor objected to Doc's treatment of the old man. Biddle waved him off. His face was bluish-white. Doc spoke softly as he continued.

"Eustus Frazier's partner returned to Texas. San Antonio, I believe. He carried on his life, investing the gold he brought with him. He slipped back, having been thought dead. He assumed a different name and made no bones about having fought in the great war for Texas independence. He left out the part about the Alamo gold—which, by the way, never got to the Alamo."

Biddle loosened his collar. His breath was not coming easy. Doc leveled a finger at the old man.

"You, sir, were Eustus Frazier's partner."

Tabor stood up. "This is an outrage."

"The key was the boy," Doc continued. "Tommy, the deaf-mute. He turned into Ezra Frazier. He knew about the treasure from a letter his aunt had showed him. He wanted someone to back him. How did he get to you, Mr. Biddle?"

The old man shook his head.

Doc sighed. "Must I say it for you? Hollis Morton came to you, asking advice about the young man who was blackmailing him. You see, Frazier traced the family connection to Morton. When he demanded money from the old man, Morton came to you, wondering what to do."

Tabor started for the door. "I'm going to call the marshal at once."

"No," Biddle wheezed. "Let him finish."

Tabor stood frozen by the door. Was Doc right? The old man leaned back in his chair, dabbing his forehead with a handkerchief.

"Mr. Biddle here contacted Ezra Frazier, telling him to continue with his extortion. Biddle figured if he could force Morton to finance the expedition, Frazier would be out of his hair."

Raider was on the edge of his seat, taking in every word. "But, Doc, why would Biddle here want Frazier to leave town?"

Doc looked at the old man. "Would you like to answer that, Freemont?"

"I thought Frazier would be killed down there," Biddle replied. "I figured he wouldn't come back even if he knew the truth."

"You showed him where to go, didn't you?" Doc asked.

Biddle nodded. "I convinced him that Morton had confided the treasure's location to me. He believed every word I told him."

Raider squinted at the old man. "Then you *are* the varmint Doc says you are. You were Frazier's partner."

"I was older than he," Biddle replied. "I had more to lose by staying down there. He was crazy, that act of letting the natives worship him. I didn't want to stay behind. I had to come back." He looked at Doc. "Where did you catch me? I must know."

"The ship," Doc replied. "The boat to Mexico. Only an insider could have known how to get young Frazier on that sloop. I wired Galveston for the harbormaster's records. Your name appeared on the log as the one who had commissioned Captain Crockett."

Raider stood up. "You didn't want us to come back. I oughta shoot your worthless hide for—Biddle? Hey, Doc, somethin's wrong!"

The old man had slumped forward onto the desk.

Doc told Tabor to get some cold water. He then opened a window and loosened Biddle's collar. Raider leaned over the old man, wondering if he had forced him to croak right there in the study. Hell, Doc had been the one needling him, but he'd decided to die when Raider raised his voice.

"He gonna make it, Doc?"

"I don't know yet."

Tabor came back with the water. Doc poured a glass and dropped a powder into the liquid. He made Biddle drink it all. The old man's breath began to ease. He leaned back and looked up at Doc.

"I knew you'd sink me, Weatherbee. I knew it the moment I laid eyes on you. Congratulations."

"You sank yourself," Doc replied. "And you're going to live. For what purpose I do not know."

Tabor put his hand on Doc's shoulder, turning him away from Biddle. "Weatherbee, what are we going to do? Do you think we should prosecute? I mean, look at him. He's an old man."

Doc shook his head. "That is not my decision. I simply reported my case. I'll file a report with the governor's office if need be."

"Not necessary," Tabor replied. "I suppose we should get him to a real doctor. He doesn't look well at all."

"He's a tough old bird," Raider said. "It took gumption to do what he did, even if it was wrong all the way around."

Doc leaned toward Tabor. "Perhaps if you talked Mr. Biddle into letting the state control his assets. After all, his wealth came from the gold that was taken during the war. If you choose not to prosecute, he might willingly sign over his properties."

Tabor's lips almost broke into a smile. "I see what you mean. Hmm, I suppose I could speak to the governor."

"Is everything all right?"

Abigail Biddle had stuck her head through the door of the study. Her green eyes were wide, her bosom lily-white. Raider felt a jolt through his entire body.

Abby bent over her brother. "Freemont, you don't look good at all. Maybe you should go upstairs and lie down."

"I wholeheartedly agree," replied Hardy Tabor. "And Abigail, I must speak to you tomorrow morning."

She looked each one of them in the eye. "Will someone tell me what is going on around here?"

"Yes," said Freemont Biddle. "One of you tell her."

Doc helped the old man to his feet. "Mr. Tabor, perhaps we should leave my partner and Miss Biddle alone for a while. Raider, you can make a few things clear to Abigail."

Doc and Tabor helped Biddle out of the study.

Abby turned toward the big man. "Raider, what's going on here?"

Raider grimaced, wondering why he had drawn the duty of telling her. When he saw those breasts, he knew exactly why Doc had left them alone. Of course, a woman could take news sort of funny sometimes.

"You see, Abby, there was this thing a long time ago, right before the Alamo. And there was these two boys that got their hands on a big passel of gold, and they was thinkin' they ought to keep it for themselves."

He went on, laying out the story for her. He was sort of proud that he told it so well. It was almost like one of Doc's reports. When he finished, Abby had a blank look on her face.

She sat down in one of the chairs. "Let me see if I've got this straight. You're saying that my brother stole a bunch of gold and started his businesses. And now he's going to lose everything to the government?"

Raider shrugged. "Well, it ain't rightly his, is it?" He slipped his hand around her waist, drawing closer to her. "Hey, don't fret about it. You're a fine old gal. And didn't your husband leave you a bundle?"

"Hell no," she cried. "I just say that so people won't think I'm living off my brother."

"Abby." He tried to kiss her.

Abby replied with the flat of her hand. "Damn you, you have to go and ruin everything. I won't have a penny to my name."

Her arms were flailing at him. When Raider retreated, she started to throw things at him. He ran out of the study, slamming the door behind him.

Doc laughed at him from the hallway. "The queen blames the messenger for bad tidings."

Raider fixed his new Stetson on his head. "I'll see you in a couple of days, Doc."

"But . . ."

"No buts. I got to do some things to take my mind off that jungle. You know what I mean?"

After a moment's hesitation, the man from Boston replied that he understood what his partner meant. Understood it perfectly, as a matter of fact.

EPILOGUE

Raider hung in the shadowy threshold, watching as the woman stripped the sheets from a feather mattress. He focused on her olive-hued breasts, which almost spilled out of her low-cut gingham dress. When the woman looked up at him she gasped and dropped the bedding to the wooden floor.

"Son of a bitch, cowboy, you want to scare me half to death?"

Raider shrugged. "Sorry."

"What the hell are you doing here anyway? My place don't open till after dark."

Her voice was compelling. She had jet black hair that showed fine slivers of white. Full-figured and round, the way Raider liked them.

He smiled at her. "Well, honey, I was just out tryin' to scare up a little fun. You'd never guess how hard it is to find a little action in San Antone, especially in broad daylight."

Her lips curled in a disgusted snarl. "Well, you ain't gonna find any of it around here. My girls is all sleepin' right now."

Raider raised an eyebrow. "You ain't sleepin'."

She hesitated for a moment, peering at him with dark brown eyes. She tossed her hair in that vain female way, like she was flattered that Raider would choose her. Finally she shook her head.

"I ain't doin' it, cowboy. Them days is over for me. I run this house now. Ask anybody."

"I asked the bartender at the Double Dollar," Raider replied. "He said if anybody could fix me up it would be ol' Kitty."

She chortled. "I ain't that old."

"No, you ain't." He smiled. "In fact, I'd say you was a pretty good-lookin' woman. Downright fine, if you ask me."

Her foot tapped on the wooden floor. "Is that what you think?"

"Yes, ma'am."

She brushed the hair away from her face. She had thin features, except for her broad lips. Probably half Mexican, Raider thought, and every bit as beautiful as the girl from the volcano.

He shook his head back and forth.

The woman eyed him suspiciously. "Are you all right, cowboy?"

Raider pushed past her and sat down on the edge of the bed. "I'm just tryin' to forget somethin' that happened a while ago. Hell, lady, you don't have to bed down with me. If you don't mind none, I'd like to just sleep here for a while. I'll pay you."

He took out a wad of script money that caught her dark eyes.

The woman peeled a sawbuck off the roll. "You can stretch out right here. But take off your boots."

She left him to undress. When he was completely naked, she stuck her head through the threshold to say something else. Her words caught in her throat when she saw the size of Raider's manhood.

"Stay right here, cowboy. Don't go to sleep just yet."

Raider stretched out on the bed, making sure his new Colt hung close by on the bedpost. His eyes were starting to droop when the woman came back. She was dressed in a flimsy nightgown that woke him up immediately.

"Thanks," Raider said as she stretched out next to him.

He touched her breasts through the nightgown. She reached for his crotch, fondling his ever-expanding penis. Raider smiled.

"That sure does feel good, honey."

She laughed. "Never let it be said that Kitty Crockett turns down a man who was blessed like you."

Raider sat up straight. "Kitty who?"

"Crockett," she replied. "You have a problem with that?"

Raider leaned back on the pillow. "No. It's just that . . . well, I was chasin' all over on behalf of a man named Davy Crockett. You ever hear of him?"

"Supposed to be my grandfather," Kitty replied. "My grandmother was a Mexican gal, said she had it off with Colonel Crockett. Took his name after that, true or not."

"You wanna hear a story about your grandfather?"

She nodded. Raider related the false tale of the Alamo treasure. When he finished his story, Kitty did not seem too impressed.

"I reckon I heard it all now, but hell, if it ain't true, then I reckon you oughta forget about it."

"You gonna make me forget, Kitty?"

She smiled, reclining beside the big man. Her nightgown came up over her head. Raider ran his hands along the soft bulge of her stomach. She spread her dark thighs, opening the dark wedge between her legs.

"Come on in, cowboy. And don't hurry. We got all day."

Raider rolled over on top of her, pressing the head of his manhood against her feminine wetness. She gasped when he penetrated her in a slow thrust. Her eyes rolled back and she moaned with pleasure.

Raider began to move his hips, initiating the process of forgetting. It would be a while before he stopped dreaming of the volcano. But at least he could enjoy himself while he was awake.